BLEAK HOLIDAY

HANK KIRTON

APOPHENIA

This book is a work of fiction. The characters and incidents portrayed in it are all drawn from the author's imagination. Any resemblance to real persons, living or dead, events or localities is purely coincidental.

First published in the world in 2014 by Apophenia

ISBN: 978-0615985954

Other books by Hank Kirton:

The Membranous Lounge (2010)
Conservatory of Death (2012)

For my Mother and Father

Acknowledgements:

All stories originally appeared in *Paraphilia Magazine* except: "Work," "White Napkins," "Reunion" and "The Story of Cilantro Rose" originally appeared in *Antique Children*, (#'s 1, 2, 4 and 5), "The Fear Detector" originally appeared in *The Delinquent* (#13) "Analysis" originally appeared in *Bitterzoet Magazine* (Nov. 2013) "Jelly" originally appeared in *Songs of the Black Wurm Gism* (Creation Oneiros, 2009) and "Black Eye Glue" originally appeared in *Zygote in My Coffee* (#111).

The author would like to express his sincere thanks to the following people: My sister, Caroline. My best friend, Audree. And, of course, Díre McCain and Dave Mitchell.

CONTENTS

JELLY

1

As far as Danny knew, he was Damon's only friend. They sat in the same class, Mrs. Arcentales's class. Damon had recently moved to Vermont from California and was slow to make friends in the chilly New England climate.

Everybody thought Damon was really weird.

Damon was small for his age, skinny and pale. His hair was long and snarled, his clothes worn and old-fashioned and too small for him. Salvation Army clothes, everybody said. Some of the girls teased him and said he wore "dead kid's clothes" but Danny never figured out how something like that could be so easily ascertained. Damon had big crooked teeth crowding his mouth, as if two sets of choppers were trying to grow in at once. He didn't talk much.

Damon sat behind Danny. Danny's last name was Brockney, Damon's last name was Brody, so Damon sat behind him.

Danny's dad drove him to school on his way to work. His dad was a shipping clerk at Tantalus Tech, a factory that manufactured plastic bottle caps. Danny's dad made him collect them. Whenever a new cap rolled off the line, Danny's dad would come home with a pocketful for Danny. "Bran-spankin' new, kiddo. Check it out!" he'd say.

Last week the caps had been white with a picture of a pine tree on them.

One rainy Monday, Danny's dad had to report to work an hour early, so Danny was dropped off way before school started. He even beat Mrs. Arcentales to the classroom. But Damon was already at his desk, the only other kid in school, reading a book of short stories by Ray Bradbury.

Danny took his seat. Nobody had turned on the lights and everything looked strange in the early morning light. Sad and spooky.

Danny sat quietly for a long time. Nobody else came in. Eventually, he turned around.

"What are you reading?" he asked Damon.

Damon didn't bother to look up from his book when he answered, "Stories."

Danny read the title aloud, "The Illustrated Man," he said. "I like Ray Bradbury too."

And that's how they became friends.

As it turned out, they had lots of other things in common. They both liked horror movies and Fangoria magazine. They both liked to draw and write weird, gross stories. They started hanging out together at recess and after school. They made big plans to write and publish their own comics and stories. They'd pass notes back and forth during class, cracking each other up.

Mrs. Arcentales threatened to separate them several times but never did.

After a few weeks of this intense, creative solidarity, some of the other kids started to think that maybe Danny was kind of weird too.

Damon started going over to Danny's house. Danny felt a little embarrassed when Damon first marveled at all the stuff Danny had in his room. His eyes boggled like he'd walked into a vault filled with treasure. "Wow, your family must be rich," he declared. "Look at all this stuff!"

"Aw, shut-up. This stuff doesn't cost that much."

"Yeah, right! Whoa, where'd you get this?" Damon asked, holding up a plastic model of Ed Gein.

"I got it for my birthday last year," Danny said. He hunched his shoulders. "It's no big deal."

"It is to me. I don't have anything this cool."

"What kind of stuff do you have?" Danny asked. He was curious to see where Damon lived but Damon was reluctant to discuss his home life. As far as Danny knew, Damon didn't even have parents or live in a house.

"I don't know. The usual stuff," he said, placing Ed Gein back on the shelf between The Creature from the Black Lagoon and Leatherface.

"Like what? What's usual?"

Damon looked around the room, gesturing with his empty hands as if trying to grab an answer from the air. "I don't know, whatever…"

2

On a cold, overcast morning, Danny and Damon picked their way through the vacant lot behind Fontaine's Shopping Centre. The back of Fontaine's resembled a post-apocalyptic landscape. Behind the stark brick cliffs of the loading docks stood a row of seventeen Dumpsters, forever vomiting the detritus and discard from forty stores. Beyond the Dumpsters, a sprawling no-man's-land of sand and limestone, crabgrass and litter stretched to the edge of a caged-off highway.

Damon had found a broken ski-pole and used it as a walking stick. He was describing a movie he'd heard about. "...And then they cut off his fingers with scissors and make him eat them. The guy eats his own fingers."

"Whoa, that's gross," said Danny.

Damon stopped. "Hey, what's that?" he said, pointing to a curl of steam rising from behind a stack of pallets.

Danny said, "I don't know. Let's check it out."

As the boys moved closer, they noticed a mounting odor, a noxious mix of sulfur and ammonia. Danny pulled his shirt up over his nose. When they reached the pallets he stopped. Damon looked at him. "What's wrong?"

Even filtered through his shirt, the smell was overpowering. Danny shook his head. "That smell. It might be poisonous. Or radioactive."

Damon laughed. "Are you nuts? They wouldn't just throw away something that dangerous. C'mon." He disappeared behind the pallets.

Danny heard him say, "Holy shit!"

Then silence, for what seemed like a long time.

Danny said, "Damon? What is it?"

No answer.

"Damon?"

Panic rushed into him and his first thought was to flee and get help but before he could run, Damon said, "Hey, come here. Look at this."

4

Danny hesitated. Damon's voice had grown slow and deep.

"What is it?" Danny said. His own voice had gotten higher.

"Just come here and see."

Danny swallowed and went behind the pallets.

Whatever it was, it was dead.

It resembled a big beached jellyfish with a face. Glutinous, translucent flesh oozed over a visible skeleton. Thin, beige veins twined like dying ivy over dormant, watery organs. Its large, lifeless eyes were cloudy, staring blindly at the charcoal sky. Its face was a melting expression of pain and fear. The acrid stench emanating from it burned Danny's nose and throat. Damon was staring at it with a look of stunned wonder.

"What is it?" Danny said.

"I don't know. I think it's an alien."

Danny looked at his friend. "Like an outer space alien?"

Damon nodded, still staring. "Yeah."

"Shit. What should we do? Go to the cops?"

Damon's stoic expression didn't change as he lifted the ski-pole and stabbed the thing in the chest.

A jet of steam rushed from the wound, hitting Damon smack in the face and he reeled back, choking, gagging.

Danny took cover behind the pallets. He listened to Damon cough and sputter for a few minutes. When Damon finally fell silent, Danny peeked out. "You okay?" he said.

Damon looked over with red, watery eyes. He exhaled a ruptured, "Yuh..." then descended into another coughing fit.

5

Danny came out from behind the pallets.

The thing had dissolved into a puddle of colorless mucus. They looked at it. Damon's breathing was labored and raspy. "Do you want to go to the hospital?" Danny asked, concerned.

"No. C'mon." Damon started walking toward the highway.

Danny followed. "You sure? Maybe we should call your parents and tell them what happened. They might want to take you to a doctor."

"No they won't." Damon was still carrying the ski-pole, the tip clinging with jellied remnants.

When they reached the chain-link fence that sealed off the highway, Damon hooked his fingers through the links and watched the passing traffic. Danny didn't know what to say. It started to rain.

Then Damon said, "I want to kiss the cars."

"What?"

Damon turned to Danny and said, "Kiss." Then he puckered his lips and made a kissing, smacking sound, as if calling a cat. Danny just looked at him. Damon turned back to the traffic. He pushed his lips through the fence, still making that wet, chirping sound.

Danny stepped back, his concern for Damon turning to horror and incomprehension as Damon's lips stretched like warm putty beyond the fence, toward the street. His lips narrowed and elongated until they resembled a five-foot-long pink ribbon and began to graze the speeding cars, still making that kissing sound – along with a soft wet thud at each brief impact.

That's when Danny finally ran away.

When he got home he was soaked and shivering. His

parents were in the living room watching TV. He changed into pajamas and crawled into bed and shivered until he fell asleep. He dreamed about drowning in a vast white ocean.

3

Damon was absent from school the next day and a sickening guilt began to grip Danny. He pictured Damon dead by the highway, cars passing without notice over his flat, waffled lips. He imagined crows diving into gaps in the traffic to pick at the puttied flesh.

When he got home, Danny found the name BRODY in the phone book and memorized the address. Damon's family lived over by the old stone quarry. Danny knew Damon rode bus 11. If he was absent again tomorrow, Danny decided he would take bus 11 to Damon's house and find out if he was okay. He had to know what happened to his best friend after he'd abandoned him. He didn't want to call. He had to see him. Damon had to be real.

His plan terrified him.

Damon was missing again the next morning.

Tension gathered all day. Danny moved through his classes like a sleepwalker hiking a nightmare. By the time three o'clock arrived, Danny sat at his desk, uncertain whether to board bus 11 or his usual number 8. The empty seat behind him felt like a malediction. When the intercom blurted out his bus, Danny flinched but remained seated. He heard 9. He heard 10. He heard 11 and rose and walked out of the room, through the front doors and boarded the unfamiliar bus.

He took the front seat, behind the driver.

The bus rolled forward, taking him down strange streets and untried byways. The faces of the kids who passed him as they disembarked were familiar but he avoided their curious looks as if they were strangers.

Eventually he was the only kid left on the bus and he worried he'd missed Damon's stop. For the first time he wondered how he was going to get home.

The bus pulled over, the door flapped open. Danny got off. He watched the bus disappear behind a haze of blue fumes and then started walking in what he hoped was the correct direction.

The road was narrow, rutted, and shaded by deep pine woods on either side.

When he found the house he knew it immediately. There were no numbers or names displayed, nothing to indicate that his friend lived there. He recognized it with an almost magical clarity, as if he'd visited it in recent dreams. The house was small and brown.

He approached the door with rising apprehension, knocked.

The woman who answered the door was gaunt and pale and dressed in black. She looked as if she hadn't slept in days. Worry-lines defined her.

"Yes?" she said.

"Hi. I'm Damon's friend, Danny. From school. Is he home?"

She closed her eyes in a slow-motion blink and pushed open the screen door. "Come in," she said. He noticed she was clutching a tattered, worn-out Bible to her chest.

He entered the house. It was dark and Spartan but the first thing Danny noticed was the smell. Sulfur and ammonia. The stink of the thing.

He followed the woman down a short corridor and into a darkened bedroom. A man with a bristling beard kneeled beside the bed, reading a Bible. He looked over at Danny.

"This is Damon's friend from school," the woman told him. "His name is Danny."

The man stood up and nodded. He was tall and dressed in black, like the woman. "Hello, Danny," he said. "I'll leave you two alone. But don't talk for too long. Damon is weak." He handed Danny the Bible. "Keep this close at hand," he said. He and the woman left the room.

Danny approached the bed and a strangled whine escaped his constricted throat when he saw his friend. Damon wasn't Damon anymore. Damon was dying.

Damon had always been pale, but now his complexion nearly glowed with a vaporous pallor. His hair was gone, his soft skull webbed with blue blood vessels. His gray, liquescent eyes bulged from pulpous sockets like some primordial amphibian. His lips were melting to jelly down his sunken cheeks and they rippled like silk when he said, "...*Hello, Danny*..." in a liquid whisper. His breath transmitted the caustic stink inside him.

Danny said, "Hi."

Silence fell between them. Danny was trying not to cry. He asked the only question that came to mind: "Why aren't you in the hospital?"

Damon shifted his head. He seemed to be melting into the folds of his pillowcase. "...*My parents don't believe in hospitalsss or doctorssss. They think they can fix me with prayersss and that book*..."

Danny looked down at the Bible in his hands.

"*But the wordsss in that book, the prayersss my parentsss keep s-saying, even what I'm saying now, it'sss just scribblesss... Meaninglesss scribblesss...*"

"This is because of what happened. That alien thing we found," Danny said, feeling stupid for stating the obvious.

"*It wasn't from outer space, Danny... It was music and light. I'm music and light... S-so are you...*"

Danny shook his head and a tear traveled down his cheek. "I don't understand."

"*I have a hand in my brain. It'sss God'sss hand...*"

"You're dying," Danny said, stating a flat fact.

"*No. I'm falling up into an ocean… It'sss a warm white ocean and everybody's there...*"

"Who's there? Who's everybody?"

"*...Everybody... Even you...*"

Damon wriggled his arms out from under the covers as if to embrace Danny. His arms were too long and soft and they flopped to the floor and burst into puddles of clear jelly and the sharp stench shocked the room, burning Danny's eyes and sinuses.

He gasped, dropped the Bible and ran from the room, light refracting to thin slivers in his watering eyes.

He heard Damon whisper, "*...Music and light...*"

He bolted from the house and didn't stop running until the road abruptly terminated at the edge of the forest.

Danny's breathing was ragged, his lungs boiling with cool fluid.

He looked at the pine tree in front of him, suddenly seized with an overriding impulse to touch the rough bark. He reached out and his fingertips stretched like upspearing tendrils until they circled the tree. He felt the whorls and arches of his fingertips merge with the grains of the wood and experienced a spiraling wave of pure pleasure so intense he was rendered blind with bliss.

Music and light. He was becoming music and light.

When the police found him the next day he'd been reduced to a smiling pile of jelly.

BRIDGETTE IN INDIA

When Bridgette returned from India, she came back changed. She also came back without her daughter and dark rumors started following her around. She moved back with her family – into that madhouse – and when I learned she'd returned I had a strange dream about her:

I'm walking across a dark, desolate battlefield. Torn bodies and limbs stretch before me, half submerged in bloody mud. The sky is thick with black acrid smoke and a dying red sun casts a murky glow over the dismal landscape. The only sound is the buzzing of flies.

And then, floating from the dim horizon, Bridgette appears.

She's nude, her dark body festooned with a garland of severed heads. She holds a sword. She approaches me, smiling with bright white teeth. When she reaches me I see that her skin is smeared with bloody ash. She says, "Hi, Hank," and kisses me, filling my mouth with her tongue and the taste of blood.

I awoke gasping and sick.

The dream haunted me for days. I called her the next week. I don't know why or what I expected. It was an urgent impulse I couldn't stop myself from following. I hadn't spoken to her in almost twenty years.

About Bridgette Blake: Bridgette Blake lived on Indian Run Road, four addresses down from the small green house where I'd grown up. My parents had retired to Florida long ago. I now lived about forty miles south of Indian Run Road. Bridgette Blake was my age (36 at the time). We met when we were five and entering the chaotic shock of 1st grade. I saw her at the bus stop. She was the only 1st grader who wasn't accompanied by a parent. Once on board the bus, we ended up across the aisle from each other (the boys and girls magically parted down the middle of the bus, segregating themselves on either side). I sat alone. Bridgette sat next to Tina Feeney who was so nervous and upset about being sentenced to school that she promptly vomited – launching her breakfast into her hands as if she'd hoped to catch the gooey transgression and stuff it into her pockets before anyone noticed. But of course, all eyes turned toward the spectacle and Tina Feeney began to cry. She was still holding her hands out, strands of puke-mucus stretching across her trembling fingers like a cat's cradle.

Bridgette jumped up and sat beside me. "I'm sitting with you," she told me and laughed.

We quickly became friends.

She'd been a startlingly beautiful child with a round, intelligent face, big brown eyes, and long auburn hair that she usually wore in braids. I remember her nervous habit of chewing and sucking on the ends of her braids until they were sodden with saliva. We were best friends at first, playing together within the Cinemascope grandeur of our restless imaginations. My memories of those days are baroque and impossible, like fevered

Renaissance paintings.

As we grew, our affections matured along with our bodies – our mutual lure intensified by the kinetics of over-charged hormones. She became a stunning beauty. I got tall. She became my first crush, my first kiss, my first lover. My first love. Bridgette Blake was beautiful and brilliant and witty and the only true miracle I've ever come across.

And she lived in an insane asylum.

About the Blake family: Bridgette's parents were the first people I'd ever met to whom I could assign the word "hippie." My own parents were older and avoided becoming infected by the 60's zeitgeist as if it were some kind of druggy, tie-dyed influenza. They remained hopelessly square, clinging to conformist 50's culture like a demented Ward and June Cleaver. But Bridgette's parents were something else. Her father had long hair and a beard and my memories of him are wreathed in smoke. He'd lost his left leg in Vietnam and seemed to live his life at the kitchen table, chain-smoking Camels between hits of a joint, a bottomless glass of red wine close at hand. His drooping red eyes had always seemed friendly (in a weird, dopey kind of way) and it wasn't until years later that I learned he'd molested Bridgette and her two brothers. His name was Stuart.

Bridgette's mother Patty was a plump, incredibly high-strung woman with dark venomous eyes who could fly into a sudden irrational rage at the slightest provocation. Bridgette often sported bruises or welts she'd incur for the slightest adolescent infractions. Her mother was a cracked china teacup balanced on the edge of a glass table.

We were both terrified of her.

Her brother Casey was ten when I met him. When he was nine, he found his dad's stash of acid and ate twelve tabs of Yellow Sunshine. He didn't talk much after that and when he did, made little sense. He went to a special school called "Living and Learning" over in Ashland.

Her big brother Toby was painfully thin. His hair was long and greasy, falling into a face erupting with angry red acne. Even though he was ten years older than I was, whenever I looked at him I felt like I was looking into the eyes of a dumb child. The one (and only) time I was alone with Toby, he pulled his penis out of his pants and told me to, "Play with it." I ran all the way home.

And yet, amid this derangement and squalor, Bridgette somehow managed to grow and mature into a bright, beautiful, reasonably normal girl. The only real shock she ever handed me was when she became pregnant in our senior year and told me, "The baby isn't yours."

She promptly dropped out of school and disappeared.

And now I was calling her.

The phone rang six times and I was about to hang up and consider myself lucky that no one was home, when the rings suddenly ceased and I heard the hiss of open air.

"Hello?" I said.

And then Bridgette's voice was in my ear: "Hello?" And I realized that I actually missed her. After all these years I still missed her. Incredible.

"Hi. Bridgette? It's me, Hank. Hank Kirton..."

"Hi, Hank," she said, as if I called her every morning just to say, "Hi." Her voice had grown smooth and slow

15

over the years. It trickled like liquor.

"Um, Hi. So. How you been?"

Silence for several beats. I listened to her breathe. Then she said, "I was hoping you'd call."

"You were? Really?" I said, surprised.

"M-hmmmmm..."

A return to silence.

I said, "Sooo, I heard you were in India. That right?"

"Can you come over?" she said.

"Come over? To your house?"

"M-hmmmm..."

"When?"

"Now, silly..."

And so I did. And the whole drive over there I kept thinking, *What the hell am I doing? This is nuts.*

The old neighborhood had changed. When I was a kid, it had been populated by hard-working, blue-collar families, but the plant closings of the late 80's had hit hard. A lot of the houses were empty and falling apart – burnt-out husks that sheltered a few crack-smoking squatters and homeless alcoholics. There was more litter than lawn around them.

The Blake house was in the same abject condition. The old brown paint had peeled to a few stubborn strips. The windows had missing panes and were patched with cardboard and tape. The house had been tagged with spray-paint several times. The splintered front door sported an enigmatic, Day-Glo legend: *Spookjump 00.*

As I approached the house, the thought, How can these people still live here? repeatedly interrupted the stream of childhood memories.

I climbed the front steps and knocked on the door. It

16

creaked open and I felt like I was in an old corny horror movie.

I stuck my head inside and said, "Hello?"

And from the darkness I heard Bridgette's voice, "Hellooooo... Come in."

The house was unlighted and filthy and smelled of pot, rotting garbage and incense. I moved through the cluttered living room not wanting to touch anything. Spectral residue from my childhood seemed to hang over the dusty furniture like cobwebs.

I found Bridgette in the darkened kitchen, sitting at the same table her father had camped-out at for most of his adult life. A German shepherd lay sleeping by her feet.

She was slow to notice me in the gloom. When she finally saw me she smiled and said, "Hank. Sit doooown."

She was obviously stoned.

I moved toward the table and as Bridgette came into sharper focus I was quietly shocked.

Had I also grown that old?

She was drawn and thin, her pretty round face now sunken and filled with hollows. Her skin was wrinkled and parched, her hair disheveled and salted with gray. When she smiled I saw that her teeth were brown and decayed.

I wanted to run away.

"Sit dooooown," she said again.

"Thanks." I sat across from her. The awful smell of rot hit me again but I tried to maintain a friendly, unassuming expression. I looked at Bridgette.

A smoldering joint rested in an ashtray at her elbow.

There was a small dish of what looked like grits in front of her. She held a plastic fork in her right hand. I noticed several flies crawling atop the mysterious gruel. The kitchen was alive with flies. Her left hand rested flat and upturned on the table and a small cone of incense burned on her open palm.

She said, "Hi, Hank. Long time no see. How have you been?" and then ate a forkful of grits – or whatever it was.

"I've been doing okay. And you?"

She put down the fork and picked up the joint. She inhaled a hit and then held it out. "Ganja?" she croaked.

"No thanks."

After she exhaled, she said, "You don't smoke anymore?"

I shook my head. "It doesn't agree with me."

She smiled at that.

I looked around the room, waving flies away from my face. "Where is everybody?"

"Who?"

"Your folks. Toby and Casey."

"They're downstairs."

"Downstairs?"

She took another hit from the joint and nodded.

"In the cellar?"

"In the cellar," she croaked, holding the smoke. She put the joint down, exhaled, and then ate another forkful of gritty gray goop.

"What are you eating?" I asked.

She swallowed and said, "I don't know. I think it's cereal." Then she laughed and said, "Want some?"

"No thanks."

Silence fell for a long time and we just looked at each other. Finally, I said, "So, how was India?"

She shrugged. "It was okay."

"Yeah? Whereabouts were you?"

"All over. Mostly Barha in Khurja, Uttar Pradesh."

"Oh yeah? Is that nice?"

She gave me a strange grin I couldn't decipher. "It has its moments," she said.

"How's Candi?" I said, and then wanted to withdraw the question.

About Bridgette's daughter, Candi: She was a severely mentally-retarded child of incest. Stuart Blake raped Bridgette when she was seventeen. When she learned she was pregnant, she ran away to New York City. She lived on the streets for a few months before hooking up with a new-age cult called *The Children of Om*. They invited her to deliver her baby at their 12-acre ashram, upstate.

It was there that she gave birth to Candi in June of 1985.

She remained at the ashram for several years. The rumor at our five-year high school reunion was that she shaved her head, wore a yellow robe and begged for change in the subways. Whenever I was in New York I looked for her.

And then in 1994, *The Children of Om* made the news.

A seven-year-old boy named Hilly Cotton disappeared from his home, just a few miles south of the ashram. As the police search entered its second day, *The Children of Om* abruptly disbanded and scattered. The leader of the sect, a middle-aged guru who called himself Sri Baba Biswas (formerly Melvin Finkel), fled to India with a few select members of his flock – Bridgette and her daughter among them. Neither Hilly Cotton nor his remains were ever found, but many believed he'd been ritually "sacrificed" by the cult. Tales of black magic, satanic rituals and even necrophilia and cannibalism still hovered over the history of *The Children of Om*.

"Candi's okay," Bridgette told me. "I left her in India."

"Really? So, are you going back there?"

"Yeah. I just came home to take care of some long overdue business."

"I see." I looked at her palm. The incense had burned to spent ash and I detected a whiff of scorched skin. Both her hands were spotted with burn scars.

She picked up the joint and offered it to me again. "Sure you don't want some?" she said. "It's dynamite reefer, grown in the mountains of Nepal."

I raised my hands and said, "No, thanks. I actually have to get going." And I stretched my legs, accidentally kicking the sleeping German shepherd under the table. I'd forgotten it was there.

The dog did not stir.

Now that the incense had died out, the smell of decay had grown stronger and something hideous occurred to me. With mounting fear and disgust, I bent down and looked under the table.

The dog had been dead for a while. It was crawling with flies and surrounded by a squirming nimbus of maggots.

I don't know how I kept from throwing up. I jumped away from the table and backed into the sink, causing a stack of dirty dishes to topple and shatter on the tile floor.

Bridgette stared at me through stoned, bloodshot eyes and said, "What's the matter?"

And then I remembered her family in the cellar and realized I hadn't heard so much as a murmur or a cough since I'd entered the house. The basement was directly beneath the kitchen.

"I have to go," I told her, already halfway across the room. "I don't feel well..."

I heard her say, "Well, you want some aspirin or something?" And then I was outside and back in the clean fresh air. I drove home with all the windows down, trying to get the smell of smoke and decay out of my nose, out of my clothes.

About Bridgette Blake: Bridgette may have endured the madness and moral corruption of her family with an amazing degree of self-possession, and even seemed to triumph over her appalling legacy for a while, but I'd always detected a certain amount of sadness and wrath just below the surface, even when we were small. I'll never know the full extent of the horrors she suffered in that house on Indian Run Road, or what bizarre horrors she fled to in *The Children of Om*, and the dark, squalid corners of India. But I believe she internalized every cruel abomination she'd ever suffered or witnessed, and these vile, violent experiences slowly devoured her soul, until finally the suppressed evil inside her couldn't be contained anymore.

An anonymous tip led police to the Blake house the next day (and no, it wasn't me). They discovered Bridgette's family in the basement. Her father had been castrated, his genitals stuffed down his throat. The autopsy indicated he'd choked to death. Toby and Casey were found with their ears, noses and hands cut off, their tongues cut out. They had bled to death. Patty Blake had been repeatedly stabbed in the abdomen and gutted. Her autopsy revealed that the half-digested contents of her stomach (Rice Krispies, bananas and milk) had been removed. Police found traces of Patty's stomach contents on a small dish on the kitchen table.

Bridgette Blake is still at large four years later.

I assume she returned to India to be with her daughter.

THE STORY OF CILANTRO-ROSE

This is what a woman did.

Once upon a time there lived a gentle, beautiful woman named Cilantro-Rose who lived in a small, wattle-and-daub hut deep in a forest of willow trees. Fields of jewelweed surrounded the house – juice-filled, translucent stalks of jade reaching up from the moist, mossy ground. The soil under Cilantro-Rose was black, rich.

Cilantro-Rose slept in a soft bed wrapped in slow waves of warm fabric. When she opened her eyes in the morning she counted the galaxies of dust drifting through the angles of sunlight projected from her half-dreaming mind. She wanted to label every dancing particle with names like gothic cathedrals.

Cilantro-Rose worked as a midwife and dowser. She delivered your baby. She told you where to dig your well.

She spent her small sums of money on things like butter, flour, and Charlie Chaplin movies.

A stream behind her house kept her company. The

stream spoke to her in tangles of black sound, about echoes without sources and invisible lines that turned impossible curves. It spoke of the illusion of time. Cilantro-Rose found the stream more truthful than stars.

A mile south, where things turned dry, fallen columns could be studied and appreciated, but Cilantro-Rose, keeping her interests modest, never wondered about them.

Cilantro-Rose kept a garden. She had a cat. She hunted quail with a slingshot in autumn and gathered wild grapes and blackberries in summer. In the smoldering dawn, she fished for rainbow trout in the stream. She dropped her line under a small waterfall, so the trout were obscured by bubbles and foam. She didn't want to see the fish before she caught them. Farther upstream stood a flat-topped rock where she could sit and watch the trout dart and splash. She did not fish there, but sometimes she sat there all day, even when it rained.

One day, old Moke Hocus ran to her house, and with nervous words and surging sweat told her that A Certain Woman had undertaken a difficult, strenuous labor and needed attention.

Cilantro-Rose gathered her instruments, fed her cat and followed old Moke Hocus through the forest. They walked three miles and did not speak. She walked behind him.

When they arrived at The Certain Woman's home, Cilantro-Rose felt something writhe inside her stomach and bowels, like a toxic blossom of grease unfolding and expanding inside her.

Before she even entered the house, she knew something was wrong.

The Certain Woman's house was large and opulent and a silver-buckled servant led them inside.

From the bottom of the stairs they heard screams.

They ascended the steps to The Certain Woman's bedchamber. Cilantro-Rose could see green in the air, sickness like mist.

The Certain Woman lay trembling in her bed, bedecked with heavy jewelry, her face twisted into a mask of catastrophe.

Cilantro-Rose approached the bed. The Certain Woman's color was very bad, like a drowned earthworm. Her respiration was erratic and carried the pungent hum of dead animal smell.

"We have to get her out of the bed," Cilantro-Rose said.

Old Moke Hocus nodded and they set to work.

Cilantro-Rose ordered old Moke Hocus and the silver-buckled servant to hold The Certain Woman upright, supporting her with hooked arms, while Cilantro-Rose kneeled on the floor and parted The Certain Woman's wet, trembling legs.

The Certain Woman screamed and said, "What are you doing to me?! Where's Doctor Puncture?" and then screamed again.

"Your husband's gone to get Doc Puncture," old Moke Hocus told her. "But it's gonna take them a while to get back. I brought Miss Rose to help out in the meantime."

The Certain Woman screamed again, her body buckling with violent contractions.

"Hold her tight!" Cilantro-Rose told the men.

The contractions abruptly ceased and colorless mucus seeped from between The Certain Woman's legs, gathering on the floor in a lucent pool of reflected light.

Cilantro-Rose had never seen (or smelled) anything like it.

She reached for her bag but by the time she opened it and brushed her fingers over her instruments, it was over.

The thing that spilled from The Certain Woman's body was dead and deformed.

Cilantro-Rose looked at it – an angry, berserk knot of hair and bone and blood and one milky eye bulging blindly from the gummy tangle. A withered, wrinkled arm with fingers as thin as thread reached from the mass. A foot, small and crumpled, with four webbed toes, poked out like an amphibian limb.

Cilantro-Rose removed a pair of snips from her bag and severed the brown umbilical cord. The smell of feces wafted like death from the clipped cord. The thing had been defecating into the cord, poisoning The Certain Woman's bloodstream.

Cilantro-Rose finally realized that The Certain Woman had fainted.

"You can let her go now," she told the men. "Could you get some warm water and soap?" she said.

Cilantro-Rose washed the blood and strange substances from The Certain Woman, and then old Moke Hocus and the silver-buckled servant carried her back to the bed. She stirred slightly and groaned, but did not wake.

Cilantro-Rose bundled the miscarriage, umbilicus, and black placenta in rags, then said, "I'll dispose of this."

"Thank you," said old Moke Hocus. "What do we owe you?"

"Nothing," Cilantro-Rose said. "I don't charge for stillbirths."

"She'll be all right, then?"

"I think so. Tell Doctor Puncture what happened. I'll be at home if he needs to speak with me," Cilantro-Rose said.

During the long walk back, her hands tingled and itched and as soon as she got home, she washed them several times.

She buried the stillbirth and detritus – still wrapped in stained, sodden rags – deep in the garden, and then washed her hands again.

As dusk gathered, a full moon began to scale the sky. Cilantro-Rose stood in the garden contemplating the grave. She thought about saying something, composing an impromptu prayer or poem, but knew that the sound of her voice, and whatever meager words occurred to her would fall so short of her ambition that she'd just end up feeling self-conscious and small. Ashamed, almost.

She went to bed instead.

As she slept, she dreamed, but the colors decorating the dreams were wrong, as if painted with a madman's palette. The images quickly flickered like lightning before she could focus on them. There was no sound.

Cilantro-Rose awoke feeling fatigued, as if she hadn't slept at all.

The day was dim with sleet-colored fog, the windows bestowing only bleak, gray light and Cilantro-Rose lit a lamp and then started a fire in her small, cast-iron stove. Finding her kettle empty, she carried it outside to the pump.

She noticed what was wrong immediately, even

through the dense fog.

Her garden, which had been thriving the day before, had perished during the night. Every plant, every leaf was dark and drooping, as if strangled by sorrow. The cucumbers and tomatoes, the squash and green pods lay dry and shriveled in the dirt, shrunk to empty husks.

The only thing alive was a lean, silvery reed, about six inches long, rising from the fresh grave of The Certain Woman's stillbirth.

Cilantro-Rose pumped water into the kettle with numb, trembling hands and then ran panicked into the house. She bolted the door for the first time in over two years.

She made a cup of tea with clumsy hands – a relaxing blend of herbs she had grown and mixed herself. The tea calmed her panic but not the confused, nervous edge that the sight of her garden had instilled in her.

She tried to distract herself by keeping busy; she knitted, composed a letter to her mother, baked a pheasant pie, mended an old dress and washed the floors. Each time she had to return to the pump for more water, she kept her frightened gaze away from the dead garden and the strange, silvery reed.

By the time dusk settled, she had worked herself to the point of exhaustion and she slipped to sleep easily and quickly.

Her dreams were abstract – amorphous, colorless, without meaning or sense.

She awoke the next morning feeling rested and calm.

Then she opened the front door and saw the tree and her heart was shocked into fast action again.

The thin silvery reed had grown into a sprawling,

seven-foot tree overnight. Its smooth bark was black, its leaves silver and heart-shaped and veined.

She filled a bucket with water and then retreated back into the house. She felt lost. Confused. Trapped in a dream.

She once again spent the day working vigorously around the house, trying to keep her mind focused on the work in front of her.

By the time night came, she again fell exhausted into her bed and was soon asleep.

She dreamed of music that she could see – a flowing, bubbling stream of sound that lifted her aloft and carried her outside to the garden, the tree.

The tree had borne fruit – waxy orange apples that breathed and pulsed and sighed, creating the music that held her in the air. She floated to the top of the tree and plucked one of the warm, throbbing apples and bit into it. The tempo of the music slowed. The apple was bitter, and tingling juice dripped down her chin. The flesh of the fruit had the texture of rare steak. She swallowed, took another bite. A spreading warmth took over her belly as if she'd swallowed sunshine.

When she awoke and opened her eyes, it was morning and she found herself outside, standing naked by the tree, a black apple core in her hand.

She hurled the core away as if it carried disease and slapped her hand over her mouth. The bitter taste of the fruit in her dream was now an explosion of concentrated flavors and her tongue burned and her teeth hurt and her lungs labored with mentholated respiration.

Her head felt filled with caustic, dizzying fumes and tears spilled from her smoldering eyes.

Cilantro-Rose quickly jammed two fingers to the back of her throat, trying desperately to induce vomiting. She gagged herself for several minutes, but it soon became apparent that she was not going to throw-up.

She noticed that all the leaves had dried and fallen from the tree. Decayed fruit lay like spilled seeds on the ground.

The tree was dying.

And so am I, she thought. Poisoned by a dream.

Still dizzy, and growing dizzier still, Cilantro-Rose staggered back into the house, barely making it to her bed before the world blurred into a spinning smear and she fell into silent darkness.

She slept soundly for two days and was finally jolted awake by sharp cramps.

Her bladder felt near-to-bursting and she ran to the outhouse, seated herself, and voided a steady stream for a full minute, eyes closed, breathing heavily. Once relieved, she took a deep breath and opened her eyes.

That's when she finally noticed her belly.

It had swollen while she slept.

She placed her shaking hands on her stomach, hesitantly feeling the new, rounded contours. She stood up on unsteady legs and walked back to the house, dazed. Her heart rate had slowed and a strange calmness had taken over her. She went into her bedroom and stood naked in front of the mirror.

Having been a midwife for many years, she knew exactly what she was seeing. She gazed at the change in her navel, at the stretch marks running along the bottom of her belly.

Six months, she figured. She was around six months pregnant.

Cilantro-Rose had never been with a man. And just a few days ago she hadn't been pregnant at all.

But somehow, the mystery of this didn't intrigue her. She felt tranquil, as if drugged. This strange calm lingered for the rest of the day. She knew she should be disturbed by her sudden condition, maybe even go into town and see Doctor Puncture and she wondered why she wasn't more troubled by what was happening.

But she wasn't. She was serene, as if a vital puzzle piece that her mind had always been searching for had finally been eased into place.

That night, she dreamed of falling through an endless universe of intense, colorful patterns – merging, growing, dividing, collapsing – a vast, warm, kaleidoscopic ocean.

The next morning she went into labor.

The contractions started at dawn, waves of strange pain rising like a tide, falling away, and then rising again. Her sheets were soaked with spillage.

She got out of bed and grabbed her bag, filled a wash basin with water, and then pulled her birth stool out of the closet. The stool was made of polished oak, with a crescent-shaped hole in the seat and sturdy armrests. She layered rags in a basket and placed it beneath the stool. Another wave of contractions seized her and she sat down and began taking in long slow breaths, massaging her vaginal opening with her left hand and pushing the top of her abdomen with her right.

Cilantro-Rose never thought that one day she'd be her own midwife.

She began to push, gasping with pain and effort.

Blood rained on the rags in the basket and she felt the infant begin to pass through her wide, dilated vagina.

It was a fairly fast delivery. The baby landed in the basket after a strong push and long scream.

Drained and in terrible pain, Cilantro-Rose managed to stand on weak, unsteady legs and push the birth stool away from the basket.

She looked down and felt a crushing weight on her chest.

The baby was alive, but badly deformed.

Its head was large and bulbous, its wide, membranous ears narrowed to fine points. Its eyes were huge and black – all pupil. Its mouth looked like a soft beak. Its fingers and toes were very long. Its neck was also much too long and slender. It was a boy, and had a corkscrew penis. The child squirmed.

Cilantro-Rose pulled out her placenta and it slopped to the floor with a *splat*. She severed the umbilical cord and then sprinkled fine salt on the child to absorb mucus. She rinsed the infant in the basin, and then powdered and rinsed it again. She used a syringe to suck the thick liquid from its nostrils, then wrapped the strange baby in a towel and placed it on her bed.

She taped gauze to the bleeding splits in her perineum.

Then she collapsed to the floor in an exhausted faint.

When she awoke she, at first, thought the birth had merely been a bad dream. Then she saw the wet placenta beside her and she slowly, painfully pushed herself to her feet.

The baby was gone.

She looked under and around the bed. It was not there.

She went into the kitchen and found the child sitting at the kitchen table. It had grown while she'd been passed out, looking more like a six-year-old than a newborn. Its skin was like polished silver. It had found the bucket of garbage that Cilantro-Rose kept in the corner and was shoving handfuls of refuse into its beak-like mouth: carrot peels, eggshells, chicken innards, onion skins, congealed fat, rotten tomatoes...

It noticed Cilantro-Rose and stopped eating and stared at her with its huge, wet, black eyes. Its movements were quick and jerky, like a curious bird.

And then it shocked her by suddenly speaking: "Obnob. Gob. Ob. Nob. Nobob. Ob." After each odd word, there was a popping sound. She could see a black, undulating tongue and tiny triangular teeth. Its voice was deep, and it pronounced the words slowly.

It stopped its sluggish babble and stared at her for another minute, huge misshapen head jerking sideways, and then it opened its mouth and shrieked, "Maaaaaaawwww..!"

Cilantro-Rose screamed, ran back to the bedroom and slammed the door.

She dressed and then spent the next several hours pacing, wincing at the pain between her legs. After a while she began to bleed again and taped fresh gauze to her wounds, but she kept pacing, frantic, wishing her bedroom had windows large enough to crawl through so she could escape.

What kind of monster had she given birth to? Who could have cursed her like this? What otherworld devilry was at work here? Cilantro-Rose felt as if she were slipping into madness.

Occasionally, she would hear the creature shuffling and scraping behind the door and hear it uttering those slow, odd words, "Obnaw. Blobnob. Ob. Gobhaw..."

Cilantro-Rose began to grow thirsty. Her mouth had gone dry and she soon had trouble swallowing.

She had to get out. She had to get a drink. Besides, her lamp was nearly out of kerosene. The thought of sitting blind in the dark with that *thing* out there terrified her.

She pressed her ear to the door. There was no sound coming from the other side.

She slowly turned the key and cracked open the door. She still heard nothing, saw nothing.

She lifted the lamp, pushed the door open and stepped into the next room. It was empty.

The front door was open and a cool wind blew into the house. She grabbed a bucket and went outside to the pump. She moved slowly and quietly, looking around for the thing. She did not see it. The world was aglow with full yellow moonlight.

She started pumping the cold metal handle and water splashed into the bucket.

I made it, she told herself. All she had to do was get the water into the house and lock the door and she'd be safe. Hopefully.

She turned to go back and found herself looking up into huge black eyes and fear charged a pounding industrial machine in her chest. Its eyes reflected her terrified face in spots of gold moonlight.

Cilantro-Rose screamed and backed against the pump and the bucket fell to the ground. The thing had continued to grow and now stood at least six feet tall.

She screamed again and the thing spread out its long, wiry arms, stepped toward her...

And gave her a gentle hug.

"Obnaw. Gob. Ob."

It released her and stepped back. Its dark eyes were shiny with moisture. It looked like it was about to cry.

Cilantro-Rose felt her pulse relax. She expelled a long breath that was part sigh. "I know," she said. It was as if the embrace had erased all fear.

She reached out, took his hand, and guided him back into the house.

Her son.

When they passed the garden, Cilantro-Rose noticed that at least a dozen new silvery reeds had sprung up.

Once in the house, she led him into a chair at the kitchen table. "Sit here," she said, and began to prepare supper. She put a chicken on to boil and then set about making biscuits. Her son watched her in silence, motionless. His silver skin shined.

"Well," she said. "I guess you'll need a name now."

She didn't look at him while she spoke. His appearance still disturbed her. He looked like some dark, primeval myth.

"How about Charlie?" she said. Maybe if she named him after someone she loved, who made her laugh – Charlie Chaplin – it would help dilute some of the threat, the strangeness she felt in his presence.

"Is that okay with you?"

He sat and stared.

"Okay, then. Charlie it is."

"Obna. Ha. Globba."

She smiled at him and in response his soft beak turned up at the corners.

They ate in silence. His mouth made a wet smacking sound as he chewed and strands of thick drool oozed from his chin. He ate everything on his plate, crunching up the chicken bones with his sharp little teeth.

Cilantro-Rose cleared the table and then fixed him a place to sleep, laying out blankets on the floor. Charlie remained at the table, watching her.

"Okay, there you go. You can bed down here when you're ready to sleep," she said, indicating the blankets by the table. "Now if you'll excuse me, I'm beat. See you in the morning."

He stared.

"Goodnight, Charlie." She went into the bedroom and shut the door, making sure to lock it.

For the next couple of days, Cilantro-Rose did her best to try to understand Charlie and get closer to him. It was difficult. His hurried, unearthly growth-spurt finally ceased at seven feet. He never slept. She tried to teach him to speak something other than nonsense, but he seemed unable to grasp the English language.

"Can you say, mama?"

"Ob."

"No, no. Ma-ma. Ma-ma. Mama."

"Obnaw. Glop. Popnaw."

"Okay. That's enough for today, Charlie. We'll pick it up again in the morning."

"Ob."

One afternoon, Cilantro-Rose arrived home from the market to find Charlie leaning over the kitchen table. He was feeling the grain of the table with his long, thin fingers, crying.

"Charlie? What's wrong?"

His tears were black as ink, and an abstract painting of his sorrow decorated the table with sad black splashes.

"Charlie?"

"Obnaw," he cried.

Cilantro-Rose dropped her groceries on the table, and then went to her son. She reached up and put her arm around his bony shoulders.

They remained like that for a long time, in silence.

Then he stood up and looked down at her. "Ob," he said. "Obglaw. Bloggom. Ob." He placed his hands on her shoulders and shook his massive head. He gave her shoulders a gentle squeeze.

Suddenly, Cilantro-Rose knew what he was trying to tell her and why he was so sad.

"You have to leave?"

"Obnaw."

He moved to the door, his long legs were stiff and crooked, like broken stilts. When he opened the door, he looked back at Cilantro-Rose. She was crying now as well.

"Obglob. Dob... Mama." And then he was gone.

Cilantro-Rose went into her bedroom, collapsed on her bed, and cried for an hour.

The next morning, on her way to the pump, she saw the orchard. Fourteen black and silver trees had grown overnight, each one of them bearing ripe fruit.

Cilantro-Rose dropped the bucket in the dirt and entered the orchard. The ground was littered with dead red blossoms and dead bees. She plucked two of the

37

strange orange apples and began to eat, taking bites from one apple to the other. Sunshine filled her belly.

Cilantro-Rose had always wanted twins.

TWILIGHT FUCK OF THREE

TOMMY: When my big brother came home from Vietnam in 1973, he wasn't broken or damaged or haunted. He didn't have a faraway stare or scream in his sleep. He still smiled and joked and helped out around the house. He got back together with Wendy, his girlfriend. He went back to work at the A&P. He didn't talk about his war experience much, but he didn't mind answering questions about it either. Yes, he'd killed people. Yes, he saw his friends die. Yes, he'd been scared he was going to die. No, he didn't really hate the gooks.

ROSABELLE: I lost two days of memory before I got to Courtesy House. I was very messed up on drugs. I do not know who took me there. Or if someone took me there. I took a lot of drugs such as LSD, PCP, cocaine, heroin, mushrooms, speed and I smoked a lot [of] grass at that time. I did not drink at all at that time.

ME: Nothing seems real right now. And nothing is real. I'm crawling on the beach, exhausted, a dripping fist of seaweed.

But not really.

TOMMY: My brother hated the war protesters. That was the only thing that really made him mad. When he was watching the television news and footage of some anti-war rally or peace march came on, that's when my brother's blood would boil. He'd get out of his chair and clench and unclench his fists and go get another beer and not come back until the commercials came on. He didn't talk about it. He just got mad.

ROSABELLE: Courtesy House is run by Miss Donna Raspberry. My first day at Courtesy House, Miss Raspberry told me, "We are going to take care of you, but you have to carry your weight. We don't give anybody a free ride. You must work and follow the plan..."

ME: I'm three, seeing the ocean for the first time; it's an immense, azure universe that stretches forever. It's beautiful and profound and frightening. I don't know what to think. The words *vast* and *infinite* and *awestruck* aren't in my vocabulary yet so I can't use them.

But not really.

TOMMY: My brother took Wendy to a party. A bunch of kids drove out to the sand pits, in back of Fulcrum's Farm. They had a couple kegs and built a bonfire and I guess a lot of people showed up and everybody got pretty loaded. Some guy named Larry started in on Vietnam. Started making a speech. I wasn't there, but I heard he was pretty obnoxious about it. Talking about Nixon and the repeal of Ton Kin and Mai Lai and other stuff. My brother usually kept a cool head around people like that. He wasn't an instigator. But, like I said, there was a lot of drinking going on and my brother did like his beer.

ROSABELLE: [Miss] Raspberry said, "We are going to heal you now, Rosabelle, take off your clothes." I did what I was told. I did not know what to do. I took off my clothes and [the other members of] Courtesy House all touched me and rubbed me with their hands. There were six people that rubbed me with their hands. I did not feel healed. When it was over I felt very degraded. I did not know how to feel.

ME: I don't want to go in the water. I'm terrified. The ocean is too big, too violent, too threatening. "Come on, honey. It's okay. See? See, daddy's in the water!" My dad is out there, a dark little head bobbing in the giant waves like a piece of cork.

But not really.

TOMMY: My brother started getting really pissed-off at this guy, Larry. He just kept going on and on. I think my brother was also getting upset because most of the people at the party seemed to agree with what Larry was saying. He hated the fact that people who'd never been in Vietnam would listen to *other* people who'd never been there like they were experts, like they knew something. When really, they didn't know shit.

ROSABELLE: [Miss Raspberry] was sometimes very nice but sometimes she was cruel. They did not give me drugs at Courtesy House and I felt very sick. I could not sleep or eat for many days and I vomited and had diarrhea and my body had many aches and pains. Miss Raspberry and the other people in the group tried to heal me by touching me and rubbing me with their hands. I was naked for this. I did not know what to do and I was afraid to resist. This went on for several days.

ME: I walk slowly to the creeping edge of the ocean, holding my mother's hand. A sudden shock of cold water grabs my ankles and tugs me as it recedes, burying my feet in the wet sand. It wants to eat me. I look up at my mother, scared and uncertain. She smiles and leads me further in. Somehow, I manage to keep from crying.

But not really.

TOMMY: So, my brother finally reached his breaking point. He walked over to Larry and said, "You don't know what the fuck you're talking about." Just like that. Got right in his face and said, "You don't know what the fuck you're talking about!"

ROSABELLE: Miss Raspberry told me I was not healing because the drugs had killed all my orgasms. She said I had to "build" my orgasms back so that I could heal. I did not know what to think about this at that time. It was crazy. But I did not know what to think.

ME: I'm up to my knees in the rushing white foam. When the breakwater hits me, my mom lifts me and I kick my legs and rise up, floating. And then a big wave hits us and I slip out of my mom's hand and the ocean grabs me and pulls me in.

But not really.

TOMMY: Larry was startled at first. He said, "Who the hell are you, man?" My brother told him his name. He told Larry he was full of shit. That he didn't know what he was talking about and that maybe he should keep his ignorant nigger mouth shut. See, Larry was a black guy.

ROSABELLE: Sometimes Miss Raspberry came in my room at night. She did not talk or touch me. She sat on the floor and looked at me. I pretended to be asleep. She looked at me all night. She did not say a word or move a muscle. In the morning she said she was "channeling" at me. I did not know what to think about this.

ME: I'm stranded out to sea. Huge waves crash against me – the toppling curl, the force, the smash. They knock me down and pull me under. They grind me into the sand and hold me there. I'm struggling and strangling, turning in violent somersaults until I can't hold my breath anymore and I'm going to drown and die.

But not really.

TOMMY: My brother wasn't a racist. He didn't hold any hatred for anybody. The word just slipped out because he was mad and drunk. But the other people at the party didn't see it that way. They didn't understand. They got really pissed-off and self-righteous and a couple of guys started shoving him, getting in his face. You know those stories about guys coming back from Vietnam and getting spit on? That stuff really happened. It happened that night to my brother.

ROSABELLE: They made films at Courtesy House.

43

"Therapy films" they called them. I did not like this aspect because I am camera shy. The people at Courtesy House had sexual relations during the therapy sessions. I did not like this aspect of it either. Sometimes they filmed this. They filmed me several times while I was naked. I was ashamed of this but I did not know what to do. I was afraid. Miss Raspberry was very threatening towards me at times. I did not know what to do.

ME: I scream in terror and suck freezing salt water into my lungs and my head becomes quiet and filled with dark galaxies. My body goes numb and I think, "I'm going to die, right now..."

But not really.

TOMMY: My brother started swinging at the guys around him. I know he broke one guy's nose. My brother was pretty tough. He took two years of boxing at the YMCA. He was a good fighter. But he was surrounded and they overpowered him and, probably because they were all pretty loaded, my brother ended up falling into the fire. He landed face first and his clothes and skin caught fire almost immediately.

ROSABELLE: A lot of [the members of] Courtesy House came down with diseases. Many people had crabs too. I found this very disgusting. I came down with crabs. Miss Raspberry kept boxes of A-200 in the bathroom. At the end I came down with VD. I was very disgusted by this. I was scared. I did not know what to do or where to go.

ME: I come back to life on the beach, vomiting sea water all over myself. A big worried, bearded face is looming over me, I feel sure he's been kissing me. "He's breathing!" he says.

But not really.

TOMMY: They pulled my brother out of the fire. I know two guys who got second-degree burns on their hands. I guess I'm grateful to them, even though they were assholes and if it weren't for them my brother wouldn't have gotten burned in the first place. Somebody found a blanket and soaked it in water from a cooler and they covered my brother up. He was screaming and screaming. Someone ran over to Fulcrum's Farm and called an ambulance.

ROSABELLE: I came down with syphilis. I had many sores on my body. I was very horrified and disgusted by this. Miss Raspberry made everybody who came down with symptoms go see Dr. K_____. He treated everyone at Courtesy House. After I was treated by Dr. K_____, I did not return to Courtesy House. I was too afraid to go back. I am glad I did not go back. When the newspapers and TV found out what was happening at Courtesy House, it was a very big story. Many members of Courtesy House were on the news. Miss Raspberry was arrested. The newspapers called her a sexual deviant. I had to testify in court but I was not on the news. I was glad about this because I am camera shy.

ME: Nothing seems real right now. And nothing is real. I'm crawling on the beach, exhausted, a dripping fist of seaweed.

But not really.

TOMMY: My brother suffered third-degree burns on ninety-percent of his body. His face and chest took the worst of it. He hasn't left the house in over thirty years. He only lets the family see him. I don't think he's unhappy. He has his TV and books and music. His hands are pretty much useless. He reads a lot. He just finished reading Moby Dick and that's a long book. That's a hard book to read.

A MESS

"You are a mess, my dear," she said in her Russian accent.

"I know."

"Your organs are not happy."

I had nothing to say to that. The tests had come back.

"You've been drinking today," she said.

I nodded, embarrassed.

"Do you know how I know that?"

I shrugged my shoulders.

"Because I can smell the alcohol."

She sighed and said, "If you keep this up, you will be dead in one to three years."

I nodded. "Okay."

She shook her head. For the first time since I'd been going to her, she looked sad. Usually, she was all business – firm, implacable. No nonsense. My doctor.

"It's too bad," she said.

When I left her office, I thanked her.

On my way out, I grabbed a lollipop from the front desk. Grape.

I walked straight to the liquor store. I bought a twelve-pack and then raced back to my building.

In the hall, I passed the woman who lived across from me.

"Hi."

"Hi."

Boy, I wanted to fuck her. What was her name again? Erin? Sara? I was pretty sure it was one of the two.

Hi was the only thing we'd ever said to each other.

I went into my apartment – beer cans on the floor, rotting food on the stove.

I threw off my jacket, carried the twelve-pack to the couch and turned on the TV. It was one o'clock and *Gunsmoke* was on. I cracked a beer and the show started. It was a good one. An outlaw comes back to Dodge and visits the wife who'd thought he was dead. She'd been a grieving widow for years and now he was back.

By the second commercial-break, I'd opened another beer.

I thought about eating. It had been a while.

But I didn't feel like moving. The pain in my side bothered me too much.

When *Gunsmoke* was over (the ending was satisfactory), I went into the kitchen. The kitchen floor was gross: crumbs, stains, muddy boot prints, cigarette butts, what looked like blood...

I opened the refrigerator but everything inside had gone bad, either crawling with mold or way past the expiration date. The milk looked like cottage cheese. I checked the freezer but everything looked awful to me. When did I buy frozen tacos? Jesus.

I returned to the couch, my beer. *Bonanza* was on. The remote control felt like a theoretical object in my hand but I changed the channel anyway.

On one of my many PBS stations, I landed on a documentary on dromedaries that was soothing enough and boring enough to allow me to think and drink.

I dozed off after half an hour. When I woke up I changed the channel again. *The Big Valley* was on and I thought about writing. I'd started several stories but didn't have the energy or enthusiasm for any of them: a story about a woman who seduces strange men with her headless, parasitic twin. A story called, *Dog Food* about a snuff filmmaker who feeds children to starving pit bulls and films the results. A man and the woman he loves drink ice tea together one summer afternoon, and when she leaves his apartment she is hit by a car and dies. When he returns from the hospital, distraught and in shock, he finds that the ice in her glass hasn't melted yet and he saves the ice in his freezer and becomes obsessed with preserving it.

But I didn't feel like writing. I drank another beer. And another.

Another.

Another.

I stumbled to the bathroom and took a piss and faces appeared in the foam – yawning, screaming, laughing. Bubbling, intangible masks that lasted until the convulsive flush.

I felt like shit.

When the twelve-pack was gone, I went out to the store and bought a six-pack and a forty-ounce bottle of Steel Reserve – awful stuff, but it does the trick. Boy howdy. The street looked like a stream.

I returned home, took an Ativan and kept drinking. I took another Ativan.

Another.

Another.

More.

My maid, Valerie, came in and started vacuuming.

"Hi, Valerie," I said.

"Hi, Hank."

No, wait. I don't have a maid. I've never even met a maid. I must have been dreaming.

"Hi, Valerie! You look nice."

No. Wait.

I awoke and tipped the last of a can of beer into me. The can was a giant missile silo, a water tower, a cannon. Mmmmmm. BOOM.

I think I went out.

I woke up to another disaster. In my hand I found a paper towel stained with dried blood. My face hurt. Something was wrong with my face. I staggered out of bed and went into the bathroom.

I looked in the mirror.

Holy god.

Half of my face was a multicolored bruise. My eyeball looked like a purple grape. There was a scab under my eye.

What the fuck happened? Another seizure?

I lurched into the living room.

The two wooden crates where I store my movie magazines had toppled and magazines had spilled across the floor, even under the couch.

That must have been where I fell. I must have hit my face on the crates.

Valerie?

Shit.

I returned to the bathroom to study myself again. My face was yellow and black and stippled with purple around the borders of the bruise. That must have been some fall, I thought. I wished I could remember it. I thought I remembered an impact, but the memory was so soft and indistinct, I couldn't be sure it wasn't just my imagination.

This was going to take some explaining. I had to go to work tomorrow. Everyone would stare.

I decided I'd dope it all out in the morning. I grabbed a beer from the fridge, chugged it, and went back to bed. My eye started bleeding again and I clamped the paper towel over it and thought about a girl who didn't exist and fell asleep.

I dreamed about a

Editor's note: These were the last words Hank Kirton would ever write. He died on March 15th, 2014 at the age of 47 as a result of alcohol poisoning. He is survived by his cat. A cat he never named.

SWEETIE-PIE BEGONIA BABYHEAD

This story was inspired by true events.

She was playing in her sandbox.

Wait. Hang on. First things first.

Sweetie-Pie Slotnick had been a beautiful baby. She entered the world easily, unexpectedly, arriving on Christmas morning, 1967. Born a month premature, her mother, sixteen-year-old Miriam Prunella Slotnick, was sitting on the toilet in her parent's house at 115 Grunyon Avenue in Alabaster, Ohio when a sudden burst of fluid poured from her and scary contractions seized her abdomen and fifteen minutes later, Sweetie-Pie slid outside after a single maternal push and landed in the toilet with a bloody splash. Just like that.

Sweetie-Pie Slotnick had entered the world head first, anxious to begin. She didn't cry. She let out a strange, high-pitched mewl and gasped and squirmed and struggled in the cold, crimson water. Miriam – for just a second – considered flushing the toilet.

Instead, she rescued her drowning daughter and

wrapped her in a bathtowel. She gazed dry-eyed at the tiny pink newborn and said, "Hi there, short-stuff," in a squeaky, cartoon voice. And then it was time to introduce her to the new grandparents.

They were not pleased to meet her.

Miriam named her child, Sweetie-Pie Begonia Slotnick. Three months later, Miriam ran away from home, eventually settling in the Haight Ashbury district of San Francisco where she joined the Process Church of the Final Judgment, married a thirty-five-year-old streetmime named Paul Kindersley, acquired a heroin habit, and a year later gave birth to a son she named Luscious Barberpole Slotnick Kindersley IV.

Her parents, Edgar and Edie Slotnick, raised Sweetie-pie Begonia as if she were their very own daughter.

That is to say, badly.

Sweetie-pie developed normally in all aspects except one: her head (and the little gray brain within). Born with the rarest form of microcephaly, her head simply did not change or grow or mature. Her pudgy little babyface remained blue-eyed and hairless, toothless and cute for her entire life.

Now then, where were we?

She was playing in her sandbox. It was deep in July – searing and sticky and Sweetie-Pie wore pink hotpants and a red tubetop that barely contained her large breasts. Her hotpants bulged lumpy over the diaper beneath. Sweetie-Pie had just turned eighteen and had the voluptuous body of a 1940's burlesque stripper (and the head of a shaved squirrel monkey).

Pushing up piles of sand with her hands, stabbing little holes with her fingers, Sweetie-Pie emitted gurgling, sputtering noises through her tiny toothless babymouth.

"Fuck, man. There she is…"

Rod, Emmett and Scoop, three neighborhood boys, peeked at Sweetie-Pie from behind the fence that bordered the Slotnick's vibrant, immaculate lawn.

"Holeee! Wouldja lookit that ass!" said Emmett.

"Yeah! Phoo! An' get a load a' them jugs!" said Scoop, feeling-up the empty air in front of him with a lusty squeezing motion. "Like Candy Samples!"

"Yeah, but…" said Rod.

"Yeah but nothing," said Scoop. "She's fine."

"Yeah, but…"

"Ah, shuddup, Roddy," said Emmett. "Why you gotta crunch the fun outta everything? Shit."

Rod went silent.

"Hey Scoop?" Emmett said.

"Yeah?"

"Would you ball her?" Emmett wanted to know.

Scoop's young, freckled face turned thoughtful. He wiped away a bead of sweat from his temple and then stroked his chin, weighing and surveying the reality of intercourse with Sweetie-Pie Begonia Babyhead. "Yeah," he said finally. "I believe I would."

Emmett nodded his concurrence. "Me too. I do believe."

The screendoor flapped open and Mrs. Slotnick bustled outside. Scoop, Emmett and Rod ducked behind the fence.

Watching through the slats, they saw Mrs. Slotnick grab Sweetie-Pie's hand and pull her out of the sandbox.

She attached a short leash to the decorative choker around Sweetie-Pie's neck and then guided her toward

54

the house like a lost baby burro. Sweetie-Pie hadn't learned to walk yet and she crawled across the lawn, her calloused knees greenstained from the grass.

Once they were inside the three boys turned and sat on the ground, backs resting against the fence.

"What ya wanna do now?" said Rod. "Go swimmin'?"

"Nah," said Scoop. "It's too hot."

"That don't even make sense!" said Rod. "What about we go over to Leeman's Pond and race flameboats?"

"Eehhh..." said Scoop.

They heard the screendoor flap open again and they turned and peered through the fenceslats.

Mr. and Mrs. Slotnick walked arm-in-arm to the tan Buick parked in the driveway, got inside. They both wore hats.

"Are they leaving?" said Rod.

"Where's Babyhead?"

"Shit, I think they're leaving her behind," said Emmett.

The boys became lost in sudden thought.

They turned and regained their previous postures – sitting on the ground, backs against the fence.

"I can't believe they'd leave her alone like that," said Emmett.

"I know, right? Some parents..." said Scoop.

"They're probably not gonna be gone long. Probably just went to the corner store or something..." said Rod, already growing nervous about where the conversation was leading them.

"No way, man," said Emmett. "They were wearing hats."

"I can't believe they left her alone like that," said Scoop.

"Some parents. They neglect their kids. Didja hear what happened to their first daughter?" said Emmett.

"No. What?" said Rod.

"Ran away from home. Died from a drug overdose a few years later."

"No shit?" said Scoop.

"I'm tellin' you. They are really shitty parents."

The boys were silent for a while.

Then Scoop said, "Maybe we should check on her. Make sure she's alright."

"You think?" said Emmett.

Rod shook his head. "No way. Are you nuts? We can't go in there. That's breaking and entering."

"Not if we have good intentions…" said Scoop. "

"Yeah…" Emmett agreed.

Rod was still shaking his head. He swallowed dry spit and said, "No. Come on, guys…"

"Shut up, Roddy, you big pussy." Scoop stood up. "Come on. Let's just take a quick look."

Emmett stood up.

Rod was still shaking his head as he stood and followed his friends through the gate and across the lush, perfect lawn to the backdoor. He prayed it was locked.

Scoop pushed open the door.

The boys entered the house, the kitchen.

The house was clean and smelled of dried spice.

There was a rustling sound coming from the next room – material scraping against material. The boys looked at each other, and then Scoop led them toward the sound.

Sweetie-Pie was taking a restless nap, sucking her thumb. She was covered by a soft pink blanket and caged within a huge playpen. Decapitated dolls littered the fuzzy padded floor of the pen.

The boys approached with silent caution, staring at the strange babygiant with wide-eyed awe. This was the first time any of them had observed Sweetie-Pie up-close. She was even more extraordinary now that all the details of her physical anomaly were revealed.

A Sesame Street mobile hung above the pen, the smiling cartoon faces of Muppets turning gently in the air: Big Bird, Ernie and Bert, Oscar the Grouch, Grover. Sweetie-Pie kicked her legs, struggling inside her babydreams, and the blanket pulled away.

She was topless and the boy's eyes became riveted to her large breasts.

Scoop tried to exhale tension.

Rod whispered, "Okay, she's okay. Let's go."

"Sh," said Scoop.

Sweetie-Pie's eyes fluttered open. She popped her thumb out of her mouth. The thumb was pink and wrinkled and clean – the rest of her hand was gray with grime.

"Nice going, Roddy. You woke her up," said Scoop.

"Come on. Let's go, guys…" said Rod.

"Hey, Emmett?" said Scoop. "Dare me to feel her up?"

Emmett nodded, still staring at Sweetie-Pie. "Yeah," he said softly. "I dare you."

Scoop placed his hands on the wall of the playpen, didn't move for a full minute, and then climbed over the side.

Sweetie-Pie had rolled over on her back. She looked at Scoop with big, curious eyes.

Scoop kneeled beside her. "Look at these tits," he murmured, more to himself than his friends. He reached out and gently palmed Sweetie-Pie's left breast. She gurgled and kicked her feet.

Emmett and Rod watched.

Scoop moved his hand to her other breast and gave it a soft squeeze.

"How do they feel?" Emmett wanted to know.

Scoop nodded. "Nice. Come feel for yourself."

"Yeah..." Emmett climbed into the playpen.

Sweetie-Pie revealed her pink gums in a wide, benign smile and warbled: "Deeeee-la-da-dooo..." causing clear, watery drool to gather on her bottom lip.

Emmett placed his hand on Sweetie-Pie's breast. "Whoa," he said. "Soft..."

"Nice, huh?" said Scoop.

Rod backed away from the playpen and nervously stationed himself by the window to watch for the Slotnick's inevitable arrival.

He heard Emmett say, "Hey, Scoop. Y'wanna take a look at her pussy?" and panic spiked inside him. He cast a quick glance back at the playpen, then returned to his vigil at the window, staring at the empty driveway, anxiously waiting for the tan Buick's return.

Meanwhile, Scoop was unfastening Sweetie-Pie's diaper.

"If there's shit in here, I'm gonna puke," he said.

Both Scoop and Emmett were relieved to find the diaper clean and dry. Scoop pulled it down off her legs and tossed it aside. The boys stared between her naked legs. Sweetie-Pie squirmed and trilled.

"Wowee…" Emmett said. The shock of finally seeing something he'd only imagined up-close and RIGHT THERE left him speechless.

Scoop raked his fingers across Sweetie-Pie's thick, black pubic hair. "Her pussy's hot," he whispered. "Feel…"

Emmett cupped his hand over her vagina. "Wow. It *is!*"

He turned back to his friend, grinning, to find that Scoop had pulled down his pants and was stroking his erect dick.

Emmett almost said, "What the hell are you doing?" but didn't.

Scoop mounted Sweetie-Pie and after a bit of fumbling and off-target thrusts, slipped inside her.

Sweetie-Pie's eyes popped wide and she began to cry.

Scoop's breathing became ragged and labored and he grunted with each thrust. Emmett watched.

Sweetie-Pie's cries grew louder. Between each high-pitched wail, her breath hitched in her throat, like hiccups in reverse, "*Huh-uck, huh-uck, huh-uck,*" and then the tearful keening resumed.

"Shut-up!" Scoop yelled at her. "Be quiet!" But the loud sound of his voice only startled her and intensified her cries. "Shit," he said. "Emmett, go get some tape or something."

"What? Tape? What for?"

"Just find some tape! Now!"

Emmett jumped up and vaulted over the side of the playpen.

While Emmett rummaged through the kitchen

"Fuck. She's dead," said Scoop. "Let's get the hell out of here."

Scoop and Emmett scrambled out of the playpen just as the tan Buick pulled into the driveway.

Rod said, "The Slotnicks are back!"

The three boys started running toward the backdoor, then Rod turned, raced back to the living room and grabbed the roll of masking tape.

They were across the backyard and over the fence before the Slotnicks even reached the front door.

The boys walked down to Leeman's Pond and Rod threw the tape into the water. They did not speak and avoided each other's eyes.

Sweetie-Pie Begonia's death was deemed accidental. She choked on her vomit. It happens.

Scoop, Emmett, and Rod never spoke about that day, never mentioned Sweetie-Pie again. Their lives went on pretty much as expected.

But Rod never forgave his friends for destroying something beautiful.

THE FEAR DETECTOR ©

One gloomy Sunday morning, an amateur inventor named Stanley Bebble finally finished building his greatest invention: a device that measured the levels of fear in people. It was about the size of an old transistor radio, with a small, curved, platinum antenna. Its delicate, highly-sensitive sensors had been constructed based on his exhaustive research into animal predatory instincts and existential angst. On one side were the controls – a series of small black dials – and on the other was a six-stage light-meter that ran from white (no fear) to red (consumed with fear).

He'd painted it peach, and decorated it with small decals shaped like stars.

Anxious to test his new invention, Stanley slipped it into his coat pocket and hit the streets.

He kept a protective right hand over it like a paranoid gunslinger.

He'd set the controls so that his own fear would not set it off.

His neighbor, Milton Karbowski, out for his Sunday stroll, said, "Hey Stanley, how's it going?" He was smiling, carrying a cup of Starbuck's coffee and a fat Sunday paper.

"Hi," Stanley said. He quickly pulled out the Fear Detector© and read the meter. His neighbor registered orange (extremely afraid). Wow. That was a surprise. Milt always seemed so relaxed and happy.

Next, Stanley sidled up to a calm-looking old woman standing at a bus stop. She read red (consumed with fear).

Strange, she looked so placid and lost in thought and didn't even notice him. What was she so afraid of?

It continued like that for most of the day – everyone he tested registered surprisingly high on the Fear-Scale©.

A group of nuns filing out of an art museum were all within the yellow (very afraid) to orange (extremely afraid) to red range.

Every child Stanley tested was yellow, every teenager ranged from blue (afraid) to red.

How could this be? Was everyone walking around in a constant state of fear? Did they even realize it?

After several hours of similar results, Stanley grew tired and depressed and decided to call it a day. Perhaps the world wasn't ready for his invention.

And then a man in a business suit stopped on the corner to light a cigar and Stanley decided to try his Fear Detector© one last time. He crept up behind him, waited for the man's Fear-Frequency© to enter the machine and then checked the meter.

It was white (no fear).

Stanley was astonished. Finally! Eureka! He'd found someone who harbored no fear whatsoever. Fascinated, Stanley tapped the man on the shoulder, introduced himself and struck up a conversation.

And the guy turned out to be an asshole.

JANET PEPPER, GIRL DETECTIVE
THE MYSTERY OF
THE KITCHEN CABINET

by
Margaret Dunnigan Dunphy
Authoress of Janet Pepper, Girl Detective: The Clue of
the Whistling Elk, Janet Pepper, Girl Detective: The
Secret of the Black Linen & Others

CHAPTER I

A Walk in the Park

"Golly, I feel peculiar! Ever since I woke up this morning,
I've felt like something odd is going to happen."

Janet Pepper, a dark-haired, petite girl of fifteen,
spoke this thought aloud as she made her way across
Bingham's Park. Her sparkling blue eyes admired the
beautiful tulips that had just begun to bloom along the
sides of the path. She enjoyed reading in the park on

sunny Sunday mornings and she carried her favorite book, *The Valley of Fear* by Sir Arthur Conan Doyle, looking for a place to sit. But every park bench she examined was still wet with heavy morning dew.

"Well, gee! I guess I'm just going to have to accept the fact of a dewy bottom," she said resignedly, seating herself on a wet, wooden bench. "Eek!" she exclaimed, feeling the cold water soaking through her sapphire-blue floral swing skirt.

She opened her book and began to read. However, as she moved her eyes across the page, she realized that the words were not registering in her mind, for she was distracted by a strange, uneasy feeling.

"Golly, what on earth is the matter with me today?" she asked herself with consternation.

Janet snapped the book shut and gazed upon the cover. The painted visage of Sherlock Holmes, Sir Arthur Conan Doyle's famous detective, looked up at her. She had been given the book as a reward for her help in solving a baffling mystery and she suddenly perked up. "I know what's wrong with me!" she declared enthusiastically. "I'm simply aching for another adventure! I need a new mystery to solve!"

Janet Pepper stood up, peeled the soggy material away from her damp rump and started walking again.

"Leaving so soon, Janet?" said a girl's voice behind her.

Janet gasped and turned to see Laura Hamilton walking toward her, beaming a bright, friendly smile. Laura, a classmate of Janet's, was a pretty girl, fair of skin, with comfortable brown eyes. She was wearing a brown and white checked day dress and a scalloped black Juliet cap over a mop of unruly blond hair. Laura was new to the town of Pinecrest Heights, her family having moved there only two months ago. Her father, Mr. Bradley Hamilton was the new math teacher at Pinecrest High and many of the female students thought he was a real "dreamboat." Janet Pepper would be mortified to admit it, but on more than one occasion, she remarked to herself that he looked a lot like Jeff Chandler.

"Jeepers, Laura!" Janet said laughingly, placing her hand over her heart. "You gave me a fright!"

Laura shared in Janet's laughter and said, "Gosh, I'm sorry, Janet. I didn't mean to startle you!" Her eyes twinkled mischievously. "I was just heading home when I saw you and I decided it was high time I invited you over for tea and cookies. What do you say Janet, are you hungry?"

"Am I!" Janet exclaimed with evident pleasure. "You bet I am!"

"Great! Let's go! I can't wait for you to meet mother," Laura said proudly.

CHAPTER II

The Hamilton Home

"Mother, I'm home!" Laura called out upon entering her house. "I brought along a friend I'd like you to meet."

When it became apparent that no response from her mother was forthcoming, Laura began to dart from room to room, looking for her.

Janet, always proper and polite, waited by the kitchen

door for formal introductions.

Laura breezed back into the kitchen and a fretful look crossed her delicate face. "She's not home. That's strange. I wonder where she's gone..."

Janet felt a sudden tug of excitement. Perhaps this was the mystery she'd been looking for.

"Oh well," Laura said with a resigned sigh. "She'll be back soon, I'm sure. Come on, let's go into the sun parlor and listen to the hi-fi. I have the new Perry Como record."

"*Don't Let the Stars get in Your Eyes?*" Janet inquired hopefully.

"The very one!" Laura said and both girls erupted into giddy squeals of excitement.

CHAPTER III

Under the Sink

"Have a seat," said Laura. "Make yourself at home."

"Thank you," Janet said courteously. She sank down upon the plush, beige davenport. "Laura, I simply adore your home. It's so, so, *sophisticated!*"

"Yes, I know. Father's so very proud of this house."

Suddenly, they heard the slow approach of a car engine and Laura ran to the window. "Holy avocados! Here's father now and he's driving a brand new car! Gee, it looks like a dream!" she enthused, swooning. "Excuse me, Janet. I'll be right back."

Janet stood up. "Yes, of course." She watched Laura dash out of the room and a few seconds later, she heard the front door open and close.

Janet was still wondering what had become of Laura's mother as she crossed to the window and looked outside. Mr. Hamilton stood lighting his pipe next to a new "Robin's Egg Blue" Cadillac. He was dressed casually in a white golf shirt and black Oxford slacks and Janet felt funny seeing her math teacher without his suit and black tie.

Laura ran up to her father, kissed his cheek and then began to talk excitedly, gesturing toward the car with her small, fluttering hands, while he nodded and smiled and puffed his pipe.

Suddenly, Janet heard a sharp *thud!* from the kitchen and, startled, she turned around.

"Hello?" she said nervously. "Mrs. Hamilton?"

The house was quiet again. Janet padded carefully into the kitchen. "Hello?" she repeated and then remained stock-still, listening.

There was a low scuffling sound coming from the cabinet under the sink and Janet's first thought was, "Oh my, it sounds like they might have a mouse in the house."

The sound ceased when Janet reached for the handle of the cabinet. She pulled open the door and gasped at what she found.

A pale young girl, naked but for white, knee-high cotton socks, was bound with heavy rope and lashed to a copper pipe. A red gingham scarf had been tied around her mouth, gagging her. She looked up at Janet with squinting, tear-filled hazel eyes.

"Mmmmmfff. Mmn. Mmrm," she said mutedly.

"Jeepers!" Janet exclaimed. "Don't you worry, I'm going to get you out of here," she said with the gutsy determination she was known for among the other amateur sleuths at Pinecrest High.

Suddenly, Laura and Mr. Hamilton were beside her. Janet had been so distracted by the naked girl under the sink, she hadn't heard them enter the house.

"That's Colleen," Laura told her, slamming the cabinet shut. "She's being punished. Right daddy?"

"That's right, princess," Mr. Hamilton said, drawing on his pipe. "And if your little friend here doesn't want to be punished as well, I suggest she keep her pretty mouth shut about what she's just seen. What about it, Janet. Can I count on you to keep our little secret?"

Janet took several steps back, trying to maintain a modicum of composure. For the first time she was grateful for the months of charm school she'd been forced to endure as she summoned all of her poise and grace to say, "Yes, certainly Mr. Hamilton. I won't say a word. It was very nice to see you again. Thank you, Laura and... Good day!"

When she reached the door, Janet pushed it open and ran outside. She didn't stop running until she was safe at home.

CHAPTER IV

A Cold Supper

"You're awfully quiet tonight, Janet. Something troubling you?" asked Janet's father, Carleton Pepper, helping himself to another dollop of mashed turnips.

"Um, no. I'm fine," Janet said morosely, listlessly

poking at the peas on her plate with her fork. She had hardly eaten a thing and her food had gone cold.

"You can't fool me, kitten. I can tell something's wrong," Carleton Pepper said with a troubled frown.

Indeed, as a former prosecutor and now Pinecrest Height's most savvy city councilman, Carleton Pepper was as sharp and discerning as they come. There were many unhappy men sitting behind bars and cold stone walls whose defense attorneys had made the mistake of underestimating him.

Janet had become Carleton Pepper's only child after her brother Ben drowned in a vat of eggnog while working at Fulcrum's Dairy, ten years ago. Her mother passed away a year later after a long, debilitating battle with cowpox.

Following the deaths of her mother and brother, Janet had taken it upon herself to become as brave and efficient as possible. She began to take an interest in her father's cases, leading her father and his colleagues to declare Janet as clever as she was pretty.

Only last winter she had taken it upon her narrow, porcelain shoulders to solve a difficult case that had flummoxed several of Pinecrest Height's most capable legal minds. When no one could figure out what had become of little Billy Eagleton, Janet, in an effort to help Abraham Sholes and Edna McCaffery, had taken over the search herself. Her thrilling adventures, which included an encounter with a mentally-deficient child-napper named Dorling Groote, are told in the second volume of this series, entitled, "The Secret of the Big Hairy Hands."

Her encounter at the Hamilton home had disturbed her but she wasn't ready to tell her father about it just

71

yet. She kept seeing that poor girl trapped in the cabinet and sometimes her mind played tricks on her and she saw *herself* naked, gagged and trussed to the copper pipe under the sink.

"I was just thinking, I have a lot of homework to do. May I please be excused?"

Carleton Pepper slid a slice of ham into his mouth, chewed and swallowed, and then said, "Well, okay Janet. But if you need to talk, I'm all ears. I'll be in the den."

"Thank you, father."

Lulabelle, the Pepper's colored housekeeper bustled into the dining room and began to clear Janet's dishes.

"Lawdy, lawdy Mizz Janet, you ain't hardly touched yo' food!"

"Leave her alone!" demanded Carleton Pepper. "You need to learn your place, Lulabelle."

Lulabelle rolled her wide eyes and said, "Ah knows it Mr. Carleton, Ah knows it," and they shared an uneasy laugh.

Janet nodded distractedly and then went upstairs to bed.

CHAPTER V

A Feeling in the Night

As soon as Janet tumbled into bed, disturbing thoughts and questions began to turn in her mind. After a restless and futile try at sleep, she finally gave up and, after propping up her two fluffy goose-down pillows against the polished oak headboard, she sat up and stared at the moon-cast shadows in front of her, the very picture of a pretty girl trying to untangle a particularly knotty problem.

"How will I ever get to sleep with these horrid pictures in my mind?" she asked herself plaintively. The more she thought about what she had seen, the more vivid and powerful the images became. "Gosh-darn it anyway!" She cried angrily and she leaned forward, pulled out one of the pillows from behind her and tucked it between her legs, squeezing it between her thighs with angry frustration.

And then something important occurred to her, something she'd almost forgotten. When she'd opened the cabinet under the sink, she noticed that the naked, helpless girl was sitting *behind* various cleaning products. Clearly, she'd been there a long time (or would be there a long time) and the Hamiltons would still need access to their cans and bottles of Twinkle and Duz and Soilax.

"How long can that poor girl sit in that cramped position?" Janet murmured to herself, squeezing the pillow rhythmically between her legs. "How long would I be able to remain tied-up like that without going bonkers?" she wondered and she folded back her thick, floral bed covers, suddenly feeling very warm.

A few minutes later Janet had made a decision. Mr. Hamilton's threats had frightened her, but had not deterred her in her purpose to solve the mystery surrounding the kitchen cabinet. She had inherited a tough, stubborn streak from her father and it would take more than threats to keep her from her mission, and the Hamilton house. She yanked the pillow out from between her legs, idly noticing a small wet stain on the clean white pillowcase, and then climbed out of bed and started to get dressed.

CHAPTER VI

Return to the Hamilton House

When she arrived at the Hamilton home, she found that all the lights were out; there was not a sign of life about the house at all. "Well, what did you expect? It's almost ten o'clock at night!" she chided herself severely.

As Janet moved across the driveway, she noticed a golden sliver of light coming from one of the basement windows at the side of the house.

A chill wind blew and she clutched and gathered the front of her coat, pulling it tight against her neck. With brave determination, Janet sneaked up to the cellar window and then got down on her hands and knees and peered inside.

Janet's young heart began to race as she absorbed the strange, shocking tableau before her.

Mr. and Mrs. Hamilton were standing on either side of the girl from under the kitchen sink. The girl had been blindfolded with what looked like a swatch of orange gabardine and was hanging from the ceiling by two chains attached to shackles around her slim, delicate wrists.

Mrs. Hamilton wore an expensive mink stole draped over her shoulders and nothing else. Mr. Hamilton wore a strange black leather get-up – some kind of harness covered with a confusion of buckles, loops and spiked, stainless-steel rivets. Below a tight, leather waist-cinch

Janet could see a metal ring around Mr. Hamilton's masculine attributes, squeezing him so tightly that his manly organs had turned an about-to-burst purple.

"I imagine my face looks about that shade right now!" Janet declared breathlessly.

Mrs. Hamilton handed her husband a thin black riding crop and he donned a leather face mask that had a shiny silver zipper over the mouth. He moved behind the girl and began to whip her bare buttocks. Janet could hear each lash of the crop, accompanied by a cry from the girl and she rotated her hips and leaned closer to the window to better see and hear the distressing scene taking place before her.

"Well, well. If it isn't Janet Pepper, girl detective."

Janet gasped and jumped to her feet. Laura Hamilton was standing in front of her. She held a revolver in her right hand and a devious smile played over her full, red lips.

"L-Laura..." Janet stammered nervously. "I...I was just..."

"So, you want to see what my parents like to do, do you?"

"N-No!" Janet insisted hotly.

"I think you do," Laura suggested sharply. "Come on. Let's go inside. I never did introduce you to mother."

Laura kept the barrel of the revolver pressed firmly against Janet's back as they marched into the house and down the cellar staircase. "Well, I'm certainly in a pickle now!" Janet thought nervously. "When Laura and I were sitting side-by-side on the box-social planning committee, I certainly never envisioned a scenario such as this!"

When they reached the bottom of the staircase, the

sharp sound of the riding crop smacking exposed flesh ceased and Mr. Hamilton turned toward the girls. He unzipped the mouth on the leather mask and said, "Is that Janet Pepper I see?"

"Yes, daddy," Laura said sweetly. "I found her snooping outside."

"Nice work, princess. Now run along and leave her to me. It's way past your bedtime."

"But daddy..." Laura started to protest.

"Don't pout, honey. Tonight's a school night. You need your sleep."

"Yes sir," Laura groused. Then she stomped back upstairs.

Mr. Hamilton fixed his gaze upon Janet and shook his head. "And you, young lady. What are you doing out so late? I do believe you have a test on integers tomorrow morning. Or did you forget?"

"No sir, I didn't forget. I studied last night," Janet insisted proudly.

"Would you like something to snack on?" inquired Mrs. Hamilton politely.

"No thank you, ma'am."

"Nonsense. Let me fix you a little something," she said cheerily and then walked upstairs.

"So," said Mr. Hamilton, peeling off his leather mask to reveal a red and hectic face. His usually neatly-combed salt-and-pepper hair was mussed and sticking straight up. "What are you doing here?" he asked.

Janet stepped forward and pointed to the girl hanging from the chains. "I came to rescue her!" she told him defiantly.

"Rescue?"

"Yes, you beast!" she cried angrily.

Mr. Hamilton turned to the girl. "Did you hear that Colleen? Janet Pepper, girl detective, came here to rescue you. Isn't that sweet?"

Colleen moaned and nodded.

"Okay," said Mr. Hamilton with a shrug. "Consider her rescued." And with that he produced a key and unlocked the shackles around Colleen's wrists. She collapsed to the dusty concrete floor. "You're free to go Colleen," he said. "Be sure and thank Miss Pepper."

Colleen stood shakily to her feet, her pretty hazel eyes cast down. "Thank you," she murmured softly and then limped up the stairs.

"There," said Mr. Hamilton with satisfaction. "She's rescued."

Janet couldn't help noticing that Mr. Hamilton's *thing* had become engorged and was sticking straight up like a long, grotesque mushroom.

"I see you've become aware of my phallus," he said firmly.

"It's disgusting!" Janet exclaimed,

"Yes, I know. Come here."

"Wh-what?" Janet stammered, confused.

"Well, now that you've rescued Colleen, I need a new girl to take her place," he said with arrogant assurance.

"Y-you mean..."

"Exactly." Mr. Hamilton seized Janet's arms and, twisting them behind her back, moved her toward the chains and shackles.

Mrs. Hamilton returned carrying a tray. "I'm back! I brought yummy fig newtons and root beer floats!" she said enthusiastically.

CHAPTER VII

A Surprise Gift

Early morning sun began to fill the dark cellar and Janet turned her face to the light. How long had she been chained up here? She didn't know. Time had become confused – a mad jumble of intense pain and pleasure followed by long periods of boredom and silence. But she would endure. Her stamina and willpower were two things that had made her one of the most admired sophomores at Pinecrest High. When people talked about Janet Pepper, after they mentioned how pretty she was, they usually talked about her resolve and determination.

"X," she quickly reminded herself. "My name is X now. My name is X. My name is X. My name is X..."

At dusk she finally heard her Master's footsteps coming down the stairs and her heart began to pound with eager excitement.

Janet knew better than to address him.

Bradley Hamilton didn't say a word as he unlocked the shackles and freed Janet from the chains.

Before she had time to regain the circulation in her tingling arms, Mr. Hamilton grabbed her left hand and pulled it toward him. He held up a beautiful aquamarine ring. "I'd like you to wear this," he told her soberly. "I've decided it's time for you to return to your father and your studies. Accept this ring as a token of my trust. I trust you will not reveal what has gone on between us. And I trust you will always be faithful to me, your Master."

Janet's throat was starting to close up and tears welled shiny and bright in her pretty blue eyes.

"Yes sir," she said submissively. "Thank you."

"I have something else to give you. A symbol of your obedience to me," he said, just before he fired-up an acetylene torch and began to heat a branding iron.

CHAPTER VIII

Home Again

Janet Pepper strolled into the kitchen to find her father sitting at the table, his handsome face wan with worry. "Janet!" he cried with surprise and relief. "Where have you been?"

"Oh, you know me, always hot on the trail of a new mystery," Janet replied.

"But you've been gone for a week!"

"I'm sorry father, I didn't mean to worry you. When I sink my teeth into a new case, I just lose track of the time."

"Boy, I'll say! The police have been combing Boxer's woods for days. They even dragged Indigo Lake looking for your body!"

"Oh daddy, such a fuss!" Janet chirped and laughed.

Carleton Pepper shared in her amusement. Then he said, "So, did you solve the case?"

Janet nodded and grinned. "Yes, you could say that."

"Well, sit down. Tell me all about it."

The thought of sitting on her newly-branded backside sent shivers of excitement shooting through Janet but she didn't want to cry out in front of her father. "I'll tell you later. I think I'm going to catch up on my sleep. I'm exhausted," she told him truthfully.

"Too tired for another mystery?"

Janet smiled slyly. "I'm never too tired for another mystery. In fact, I'm aching for another one right now!"

Indeed, Janet's adventures were only beginning. Before long she'd be off on another thrilling case, equally as strange and baffling as the one she'd just solved. Readers who are intrigued by her strange exploits may follow her subsequent adventure in the next volume of this series, entitled "The Secrets of Janitor Moss."

"My daughter, the girl detective," Carleton Pepper said merrily.

Janet looked at the beautiful aquamarine ring on her finger, and thought about the gorgeous symbol that her Master had scorched into her pretty, young flesh. "Oh Daddy," she said. "I'm a lot more than that!"

THE END

Margaret Dunnigan Dunphy was born on July 7th, 1907 in
Tarweather, Nebraska. The daughter of an eggplant farmer and
one of thirteen children, she went to work for *The Tarweather Blade*
as a printing press operator at age seven where she lost two
fingers to extra editions. She never married, but wrote fifty-seven
Janet Pepper Mysteries between 1940 and 1955 while working as
a stenographer for the FBI. She died on October 23rd, 1967 by
her own hand.

WHITE NAPKINS
by
Alfred Henry

I remember him well, an older man, maybe in his early sixties, his face worn and sad. He moved slowly. He'd walk into the bar, wearing his old gray trench coat and strange hat, walking as if burdened by the weight of his own organs. He came in every day for four days at exactly the same time (2:00 p.m.) and, unless it was taken, sat on the same barstool – In the corner, against the wall. It was 1988 and I was still in college, bartending part-time at a dive called The Dead Tulip. He didn't say much. He'd slump into his stool, order a Manhattan, and gaze at the TV without actually watching it. After a couple of drinks he'd start writing on bar napkins. After a couple more drinks, he'd pay up and stagger out, leaving the napkins behind. He did this, as I said, for about four days and then I never saw him again.

But I saved the napkins...

1st napkin: A thousand chimpanzees roar their approval as the sun disappears behind a symphonic eclipse. A vast landscape of broken glass stretches before a weary goatherder, jeweled and glinting and he without his sandals.

The broken sky has not held a cloud in two-hundred days and parched, sun-scorched multitudes moan toward heaven.

Whenever someone tried to talk to him, he would nod, say nothing, and then turn back to the TV. He didn't seem interested in sports...

2nd napkin: A child sitting in the dust sweats, and each droplet contains a tiny slow-motion film-clip of his life. Eating applesauce with Mommy. Playing catch with Daddy – his awkward, still-new child-hands struggling with the size and shape of the yellow rubber ball. His grandma dying in her diseased bed, transmitting fear and grief through her clutched, withered hands.

His printing was neat and tiny, standard cartoon block lettering. Sometimes he'd doodle odd symbols on the napkins. But mostly he just wrote prose...

3rd napkin: The goat-herder frowns and turns back. There is no water here. His last remaining goat bleats weakly and collapses onto a bed of broken glass. The goat-herder shakes his head but there is no time to mourn. He marches on.

Decayed skyscrapers line the horizon like dead sentries. The chimpanzees scream as the sun returns. People report hearing thunder, of seeing an approaching storm, but it is all rumor and hallucination.

4th napkin, 2nd day: A slender woman dressed only in a tattered slip happens upon a field of kitchen appliances. She searches through them. All the blenders are broken.

A man who used to be a surgeon dissects dead children and finds strange things in their stomachs: bottle caps, coins, flashbulbs, and shards of old credits cards. He places the items in a small paper sack and gloats over them.

5th napkin: A young man who has lived solely on a diet of starfish and raisins scratches equations in the dirt which prove the existence of God. And then dies. Two days later, a tired caravan passes through, erasing his work.

Bodies hang from silent telephone poles, their rotted flesh pecked at by screeching crows and seagulls. Birds flourish here.

An old woman studies the blue veins in her legs. She believes they are a roadmap to the afterlife, but the way they scatter into endless directions sends her a fearsome message. She cannot sleep.

He never ate. The food at the Dead Tulip was lousy, but he never tried it...

6th napkin, third day: A man pinches lice from his beard and feeds them to his son. The boy's outstretched tongue is always begging, his face an unending expression of need. The man will never shave again.

A little girl plays with a severed hand by the side of a crumbling road until her mother makes her put it down. The mother scolds the child and tells her the hand is dirty and dangerous. The mother examines the hand and then yanks the gold wedding band from the ring finger.

7th napkin: A man has an erotic liaison with a beautiful

blond woman every day at two p.m. He stares up at her. She is wearing a red dress and holding a glass of wine. The billboard is worn and some of it is missing but he ejaculates into the dirt every time.

An infant cries abandoned, skin blistered and peeling, dying of dehydration. If he hadn't been abandoned, he would have become an inventory clerk.

A man who lives in a rusted tow-truck sees a badger.

He was quite drunk after writing the seventh napkin and I had to shut him off. His behavior wasn't getting out of control, he just looked close to passing-out. He showed no emotion, didn't object, and left without incident...

8th napkin, 4th day: A choir of burn-victims sing Missa sine nominee by Giovanni Pierluigi da Palestrina, and fuck it up.

A middle-aged man finds a dead mermaid washed up on the beach, tangled in seaweed. Upon closer inspection, he realizes it's not a mermaid but a drowned hermaphrodite who looks remarkably like Carmen Miranda. He gently lifts her, carries her behind the rocks and then fucks her while thinking about the movie, Copacabana.

A man with an erased face stares at a dead TV. He doesn't understand what people saw in those things.

A chronic alcoholic strings a bunch of apocalyptic images together and tries to be funny.

And the goat-herder trudges onward, goatless.

After this last napkin, he left The Dead Tulip and never returned. Nobody knew who he was or where he came from. Joe

Stromboli, a regular at the bar, said his name was Alfred Henry and that he was a traveling salesman.

But Joe Stromboli was always full of shit.

REUNION

"Y'know why you're doing this?"

"Why?"

"Because you're a filthy sewer-hole."

"Okay."

"So, why you doing this?"

"Because I'm a filthy sewer-hole."

"That's right. Now, look in the camera and say, `Mom, I'm a filthy sewer-hole.'"

"Mom..."

"Look in the camera."

"Mom, I'm a filthy sewer-hole."

"That's right. Good. Now, open your mouth."

* * *

Webster, Massachusetts

Ben Henderson stood at the window, sipping a tepid cup of Sanka, watching for snow. A storm was coming and the tombstone-colored sky looked set to unload. The air outside was charged and tense, as if impatient to turn.

He'd volunteered to pick Amy up at the airport but she'd already arranged for a rental car. She was finally coming home after three missing years in California.

During those years, all Ben and Ruth had gotten from their daughter was one Christmas card without a return address and two brief, awkward telephone calls telling them she was "fine" and "doing good," that she was, "making money" and would "visit soon."

Ben felt anxious and distracted, as if he'd be meeting Amy for the first time rather than greeting the daughter he'd known and loved for twenty-one years.

Ruth came into the living room and said, "Might be a good idea to bring in some extra firewood."

Ben nodded.

"I said it might be a good idea to bring—"

"I heard you," Ben said. "I'll do it."

He carried his cup into the kitchen, dumped the last of his Sanka into the sink, and then returned to the window.

* * *

"What's your name, sweetie?"

"Cherry Meadows."

"Well, hello there, *Cherry Meadows*."

"Hi."

"Do you know what we do here?"

"Oh, yeah."

"Yeah? How does that make you feel?"

"It turns me on."

"Yeah?"

"Yeah. I'm getting so wet and horny right now..."

* * *

Amy Jill Henderson drove her rented Infiniti slowly, sipping her second Dunkin' Donuts coffee and wishing she'd had the guts to smuggle her stash onto the plane. Coffee was a poor substitute. Her mind still felt sluggish and stark – a gray space drained of shades. Her weariness was an ache, a weight. She hadn't been up this early in years. She lit the last cigarette she'd be able to smoke all day.

It was eight-thirty, Sunday morning. When she passed the *Welcome to Webster* sign, she felt a ripple of excitement move through her and her eyes began to shift from the windshield to the side windows, taking in an edged procession of mournful childhood landmarks.

The neighborhoods looked deserted – the lawns dead and frozen. Her Infiniti was the only car on the road and she felt safe and protected within the moving metal shell of music and heat.

She passed her friend Mary Sousa's house, where she'd seen Mr. Sousa put his fist through the wall during a fight with Mary's mom while she and Mary were trying to play Candyland on the living room floor. There was the section of sidewalk where she'd sprained her arm falling off her first two-wheeler. She passed the alley between the 7-11 and a ramshackle wooden fence where seven-year-old Billy Persky had pulled down his pants to show a fascinated, six-year-old Amy her first real-live penis.

And then there was her parent's house. *Oh God.* She pulled into the driveway, stopped, and stared at her old home. It looked different, diminished, like a flawed drawing copied from a treacherous memory. She suddenly realized it had been painted a different color –

from blue to yellow – and this realization energized her a little. They'd both changed.

She finished her final cigarette, stubbed it to death in the ashtray.

When she opened the car door a freezing breeze slapped her and she emitted a shocked, *"Jesus!"* and stepped into the wind. Three years in LA had weakened her resilience to the arctic bite of winter in New England.

A shrill voice said, "Hiiii!"

Amy walked toward her mother, holding her coffee cup with both hands.

* * *

"Do your parents know what you do?"

"No. Oh, shit no! Are you crazy?"

* * *

Even before Ben Henderson watched his daughter climb out of the car, his wife had opened the front door. He felt the cold draft and could almost see his hard-earned heat being sucked into the stratosphere.

"Hiiii!!!" he heard his wife shriek, trundling across the lawn with her arms outstretched like a big awkward bird. He watched mother and daughter embrace and then quickly moved to his recliner by the woodstove. He turned on the television and then flapped open a section of the Sunday paper and pretended to read. He could feel his heart working.

* * *

"So, Cherry, where you from?"

"Massachusetts, originally, but I live in East Hollywood now."

"Oh yeah? Did you grow up in a small town or a city, like Boston?"

"Small town, definitely."

"Were you a good girl or a bad girl in school?"

"Bad girl, definitely."

"Were you a cheerleader?"

"Oh, yeah."

"Yeah? I bet you were one hot little cheerleader. Did you ever fuck any of the football players?"

"Oh yeah."

"Yeah?"

"Yeah. I fucked them all."

"*`I fucked `em all!'* Ha ha ha. No shit. Hey, would you give us a little cheer?"

"What? Oh, no!"

"Aw, c'mon. Why not?"

"No, that would be just... *way* too embarrassing."

"Aw, just a short one. A little *sis-boom-bah...*"

Laughs. "No! Look at me, I'm blushing!"

"A little *rah-rah-rah?*"

"No, really, I can't. I'm sorry."

"What a rip. Well, let's get started. Step into my office."

* * *

When Amy walked through the door, she was hit with a broken muddle of emotions. Only the outside of the house had changed and she felt herself slipping into the past, becoming a shy little girl again. She also felt a tinge of residual teenage anger. How she had hated living here toward the end.

Her mother said, "For God's sakes, Ben. Put down that paper and say hello to your daughter."

Her father slowly lowered the paper. He forced a smile. "Well, hello there, stranger." He folded the paper, tucked it under his arm and stood up. He placed one hand on her shoulder. "Nice to have you home," he said.

"Thanks, Dad."

"Aw, sure."

They looked at each other for a few silent seconds, and then he lowered his eyes, turned, and kneeled by the woodstove. He opened the stove and began rearranging the logs with a poker. "Hope you brought an appetite," he said. "Your mother's making meatloaf with all the trimmings."

"Sounds good," she said.

"Yes," her mother said. "Meatloaf, mashed potatoes, mushroom gravy, green beans with slivered almonds, Poppin' Fresh crescent rolls..."

"Sounds good," she said again.

"Yes, all your favorites. I remember how much you liked my meatloaf. Would you like something to drink? Oh, I see you have coffee."

"Yeah," Amy said lifting her cup. She took a sip.

Her mother looked at her.

Her father poked at the fire.

Amy took another sip of coffee.

It started to snow.

* * *

"What's the most guys you ever did at once?"

"You mean, like a gangbang?"

"Yeah."

"Ummmmm... Six, I think."

* * *

With her father outside splitting firewood and her mother in the kitchen getting a head-start on dinner, Amy sat on the couch watching a gardening program on PBS. Too nervous and distracted to follow the show, she got up to check out her old bedroom.

But it wasn't her bedroom anymore. They'd converted it into a sewing room. She felt strangely violated for some reason and couldn't help wondering how long she'd been gone before they moved her stuff out.

She went into the kitchen. Her mother was kneading ingredients into raw chopped sirloin.

"Hey, Mom?"

"Yes, dear?"

"Um, where's all my stuff?"

"What stuff, dear?" She cracked an egg into the meat.

"My stuff. My belongings. All the stuff I had in my room that I left when I left."

"Oh. We still have it. We just boxed it up and moved it into the basement. We still have it all. We didn't throw anything away."

"Oh." She nodded. "Okay. Well, I'm gonna go down cellar then, see if there's anything I want to take back with me."

"Okay, dear. It's all there."

She opened the cellar door, flicked on the light. The

temperature fell as she descended the stairs and by the time she reached the bottom she wished she'd worn a sweater.

She moved across the dusty cement floor, grit crunching under her shoes. She turned on another light – a bare bulb hanging above a pull-string. In a corner she found the boxes, each one marked with the name *Amy*, written with a black Sharpie.

She counted six boxes. For some reason she thought there'd be more. She opened the top box. It was filled with old clothes that she wouldn't be caught dead wearing in Los Angeles (although the thought of attending the AVN Awards wearing her vintage 70's crochet top, blue corduroys and Hush Puppies made her smile).

She opened another box: Goth and hardcore-punk CD's, Japanese horror movies and anime, a small stack of bloody Japanese manga...

This shit could stay. She shut the flaps.

The next box was filled with stuffed animals. Her old friends. She slid the box aside. *Mr. Bobo, Miss Biscuit, Hot Toddy, you're all going to Hollywood!*

After twenty minutes, she'd amassed a small pile of things that would be going back with her: her collection of Judy Blume books, her videotapes of The Wizard of Oz and Spongebob Square-pants, a few toys, and of course, her stuffed animals.

She was about to turn off the light and head back upstairs when she noticed another, smaller box hidden behind the others.

She lifted it out and placed it on her father's work-bench.

She opened it. "Oh, wow..." It was filled with old, forgotten photographs of her, her friends, the family. She started looking through them, smiling, shaking her head with bemused disbelief. Those frozen moments seemed so long ago now.

And then she discovered the videotape and her smile dropped. Her stomach dropped. She felt sick.

Buried under the pictures was one of her movies: *Gang-banging Cum-Sluts Vol.6 Starring Cherry Meadows*. There she was, smiling up at the camera, surrounded by a battery of huge, erect dicks.

"Oh my God," she muttered.

* * *

"What do you like the least about the business?"

"The least?"

"Yeah, like, what do you hate? What pisses you off?"

"Um, the other girls, I guess. I mean, I don't *hate* them, but they can be so *mean*. Everyone's so competitive with each other. They can be threatening sometimes. Don't get me wrong, I love girls and some of my best friends are in the business, but sometimes..."

"Yeah."

"Yeah."

* * *

Amy pulled herself back upstairs, into the kitchen.

Her mother had several pans going on the stove. "Find what you were looking for?" she asked her.

"Yeah," Amy said. "And more."

"I told you, we didn't throw anything away. We kept it all."

"Yeah, thanks." Amy noticed a small pad of yellow Post-it notes on the counter by the refrigerator. A grocery list had been started. She picked up the pad and read: *milk, celery, Sanka, light bulbs, cream of wheat...*

For some reason, this short list sounded a sad, dissonant chord inside her. She absently slipped the pad into her pocket.

The clumping sound of boots stamping on the back porch and then Amy's father burst into the kitchen with the winter wind, breathing heavily. He was covered with snow, carrying several logs under his arm. "It's coming down something fierce," he said. "Bet we're getting close to two inches an hour."

Amy looked at him, trying to keep a calm expression and then slipped out of the kitchen and returned to the television.

* * *

"So, you ready for your six-on-one?"

"Uh-huh."

"Ready for an anal pounding?"

Laughs. "Uh-huh."

"And you're gonna swallow all the cum?"

"Uh-huh."

"Wait, how old are you?"

"Nineteen."

"Nineteen. Wow. Anyone you want to say, `Hi' to?"

"That's a funny question. You mean like, `Hi Mom'? That seems kind of inappropriate for this video."

"What about `Hi Dad'?"

"*Hi Dad*—oh God! That'd be so awful. So far I've been lucky. They haven't found out yet."

"Well, don't worry. No one will ever see this tape."

Laughs. "Okay."

* * *

Amy was sort of half-watching *Death Wish II* when her father marched into the room and killed the picture. "Dinner's ready," he said.

"Okay." She stood up and followed him into the dining room. She didn't feel like eating at all. Her stomach had gathered into a greasy knot after her discovery in the cellar.

They sat down to dinner.

"Everything looks great," Amy said.

"All your favorites," her mother said. "It's so nice to see you again. When you left we were so distraught, we missed you so much. Your father even tried to hire—"

"Ruth," Ben said. "Pass the meatloaf."

The meatloaf had been sawed into slices and arranged in an overlapping fan on a serving platter. Ruth passed the platter to her husband.

He forked two slices onto his plate, and then forked one over to Amy.

"Thanks."

Once the plates were filled, they began to eat. Amy took a small bite of meatloaf and wanted to gag.

"So, how you making out in California?" her father asked.

"Good. Real good."

97

"I'm glad to hear that. What are you doing out there for money? Still modeling?"

Amy ate a bite of mashed potato and nodded. "M-hm."

"What kind of modeling?" he wanted to know.

She swallowed. "Um, nothing big. Little catalogues and stuff. I also do movie work."

"Movies?" her mother said. "You're in movies?"

"Yup," Amy said. "Again, nothing too exciting. I do extra work once in a while. Sometimes I do stand-in work. My friend Mike hooks me up with a job once in a while. It's good money and I'm in the Screen Actors' Guild, so I get benefits too."

"Sounds exciting," said her mother. "What movies were you in? Did you ever meet anyone famous?"

"I was in a scene in a horror movie called *Blood Guzzlers from Outer Space...*"

"Oh dear," her mother said.

"I guess we missed that one," her father said. "Is that why you dyed your hair blond?" he asked. "For the movies?"

Amy shrugged. "Sort of. I wanted a change anyway. But it's true that blonds have an advantage out there. And supposedly we have more fun."

"How long have you been blond?"

Amy shrugged again. "I don't know. Around two years."

"I like your real hair color better."

"Oh, hush, Ben. It's *her* hair. She can do what she wants with it."

"I know. I'm just giving my opinion."

"I'm thinking of changing it again," Amy said. "Either

dye it black or just let it grow out to its natural color."

"I remember you dyed your hair black when you were in high school. Didn't work out too well as I recall," her father said.

Amy sighed. "No."

"Your hair isn't the only thing you changed about yourself," he said.

"Ben!" said Ruth.

"What? I was just pointing out the obvious."

"Leave her alone, Ben. We're trying to eat dinner."

"It's okay, Mom. Yes, Dad, I got... *enhancements.* But I did it for me. For my self-esteem."

"But it doesn't hurt your career either," her father said.

"Ben, please."

"No," said Amy. "It helps. Just like the hair."

"I bet."

"Can we please change the subject?" said Ruth.

"Okay, okay," said Ben.

They ate in silence for a while, and then Ben said, "We'd like to come visit you sometime, Amy. Especially at this time of year. What do you think the temperature is where you live?"

"Oh, I don't know. Probably somewhere in the low seventies."

"Oh my goodness. How nice," her mother said. "No wonder you look so healthy and tan."

Amy smiled. "Thanks, Mom."

"You know, I've never seen the Pacific Ocean," Ruth said.

"It looks a lot like the Atlantic," Amy said. "Y'know, all blue and wavy."

"Stop it. I know you're teasing," she said and laughed. "But I do love the ocean. Your father and I watched the most interesting documentary on seals the other night. It was so adorable, they—"

"We should talk about sleeping arrangements," Ben said.

"Sleeping arrangements?" Amy said.

"We got rid of your old bed," he said. "So, we can either set up a cot in your old room—that'll give you privacy—or you can sleep on the couch. Not much privacy, but you'll be able to watch TV."

"Uh, thanks, Dad. But, I'm not staying the night."

"What are you saying?" asked Ruth with a sudden look of concern.

"I never intended to stay more than a day. I thought I told you that."

"Yes, you did. But in case you didn't notice, we're in the middle of a pretty big blizzard here," her father said.

"I know, but I really do have to get going," she said.

"But that doesn't make a lick of sense," her father said. "Logan airport will be shut down. No flights at all until the storm's over." There was a rough edge of frustration in his voice.

Amy shrugged. "I've made up my mind."

Her mother said, "But the roads are dangerous, honey. You could have an accident. Or at the very least you'll end up stuck in traffic for hours, maybe."

"I'm sorry, but I've made up my mind," she said again. "I never intended to stay overnight. I didn't even pack a change of clothes."

Her father's face reddened. "This is stupid. You're being stupid. You'd rather get stranded in a snowstorm

100

than spend the night with your own parents."

"Sorry, Dad, I have to." Amy stood up. "In fact, I'm gonna get ready to go now. I'm sorry."

"Oh, but Amy..." her mother said.

"Let her go, Ruth. If she wants to be stubborn and stupid, let her. I'm done arguing." He threw down his napkin and then went to the woodstove.

Amy carried her plate and glass into the kitchen, set them on the counter by the sink. She'd hardly eaten anything.

Then she went down to the basement to get her stuff.

* * *

"How old are you?"

"Eighteen."

"Eighteen years old and doing porn already."

"Yeah."

"Is that what you aspired to do when you were a little girl?"

"No."

"You didn't always dream about coming out to California and making dirty movies?"

"No."

"Well, you're good at it."

"I guess."

* * *

Amy began brushing off the Infiniti, wading ankle-deep in the clean, downy snow. Every flake that fell seemed to increase her sense of urgency. She had to get the car on the road before the street-scraping plows buried the end of the driveway with heavy heaps of dirty snow, locking her behind an insurmountable barrier.

She'd forgotten what it felt like to stand in the center of a snowstorm. The moaning wail of the wind and the delicate whisper of snowfall created a kind of vacuum, muffling the hum of the world.

She looked toward the house. Her father was watching her from the window. Still pissed-off. Oh well.

As soon as the car was clean, her mother bustled out of the house, carrying a plastic grocery bag.

She held out the bag. "Here honey, leftover meatloaf and potatoes. I put gravy on both."

Amy took the bag. "Thanks, Mom."

"Are you sure you won't change your mind?"

Amy shook her head. "No."

"We're going to be so worried about you."

"Don't worry. I'm just going over to the Marriot. It's only a few miles."

"The Marriot..." her mother's face fell. "A hotel?"

Amy hadn't meant to hurt her feelings. She gave her a quick hug. "I'll call you when I get there."

"Okay. Take care, honey. I love you."

"Love you too, Mom. Say goodbye to Daddy."

"I will," her mother said, heading back to the house.

Amy gave herself a last look. Her father had left the window.

She lowered herself into the car, knocked snow loose from her shoes, and then shut the door.

She lit a cigarette and started the car.

Not much snow had accumulated on the roads and the plows were out already, but she drove slowly, slower than she had to. She was eager to check into the hotel, have a couple of drinks, and spend time in the sauna, but she drove without hurry just the same, savoring the inching distance that grew between her and her father and that house.

She thought of the short drive as a victory lap.

She smiled. Yeah, *victory*.

* * *

One week later.

Ben Henderson trudged up from the cellar carrying the box. Ruth had just left for the beauty parlor, which meant he had at least an hour to himself.

He made himself comfortable and then stretched out on his recliner. He began as he always began, with the photographs. He studied each one carefully, remembering Amy as she had been in more innocent times. He scrutinized her face, her expressions.

He spent time with them.

But halfway through the pictures, his excitement got the better of him and he decided he couldn't wait any longer. He scooped out the remaining photos to get to the tape.

It took him a few seconds to register what he was looking at.

A note had been affixed to the box, printed on a yellow Post-it:

Hi Daddy
I know what you've been doing
Amy

Ben Henderson screamed into the empty house.

103

THE GRAPESHOT BUFFET

"I do not have a prisoner to reproach me. I have exterminated all. The roads are sown with corpses. At Savenay, brigands are arriving all the time claiming to surrender, and we are shooting them non-stop. Mercy is not a revolutionary sentiment."

--General Francois Joseph Westermann to the Committee of Public Safety, 1793

The sweet reek of death hung like a shroud over the shaken, blood-stained city. He would have meat this night, at least.

Gaston Molyneux moved through the pre-dawn streets of Savenay, trying his best not to look desperate, trying not to look like a hunted man. Each time he stepped past a tangled pyramid of bodies or congealing puddle of blood, his mouth watered and his stomach screamed for sustenance.

Republican forces had been battling peasant uprisings throughout the Vendee, and butchering, burning or burying anything alive. Gaston found villages razed, their crops, orchards and even livestock burned to unpalatable ash.

On the outskirts of the city he'd come upon men unloading bodies – mostly women and children – from piled carts, dumping them into pits of smoldering bones. The smell of the fresh, roasting flesh had driven Gaston nearly mad with hunger. But he couldn't afford to risk detection by trying to talk his way into the pits or attempting to steal a burning body. The men went about their work with dark, empty eyes, as if blind to the horror in which they toiled. Gaston had a feeling that if he'd tried to approach the men or the pits, his own precious flesh would have ended up in the crackling flames. Just another carcass among hundreds.

Some of the doctors at the asylum had called Gaston a scavenger, a vulture, a ghoul. A monster.

He had tried his best to defy these descriptions.

During his journey through the Vendee, he'd seen so much savagery and dreadfulness he wondered how anyone could call him a monster anymore. How could anyone of balanced mind think him worse than those who had raped and then slain the young girls he'd seen hanging naked from the trees? How could anyone think him more monstrous than the cruel troops he'd seen drowning crowds of helpless prisoners in the Loire River, tying huge groups to sinking barges and laughing about "Republican baptisms" even as the water filled the struggling lungs of their victims?

How could anyone call him a "monster" ever again?

Gaston Molyneux's appearance surprised people. He did not resemble the famous French glutton whose gastronomic feats had been breathlessly (and exaggeratedly) reported in the newspapers. Most expected Gaston to be a slobbering, eight-hundred-pound beast, shoving live, bleating lambs down his cavernous gullet. They expected an ogre.

Instead, Gaston was a pale, thin man – shy, reserved, and polite. The only noteworthy aspects of his physiology were his large mouth (crowded with two sets of chipped, stained teeth), and the long, loose pouch of rumpled flesh that hung from his stomach, which he kept looped around his waist like a Turkish wrap.

But while Gaston may have been modest in weight and height, every molecule of his body screamed with an insatiable, all-consuming hunger. His hunger was an emergency without end.

Gone were the days of success and fame, when he'd toured Europe performing at fairs and circuses, eating heaping baskets of uncooked offal, swallowing whole apples until he'd put down a bushel, dining on rocks and frogs and crockery – all to rapt, flabbergasted audiences.

He'd been billed as *The Great Glutton of Goatland* (though if a Goatland existed, he'd never visited there) and had performed before royalty.

But *now* he was a monster?

He'd escaped from the asylum three days ago, and had been subsisting on meager scraps while he made the slow, agonizing journey across the barren countryside to Savenay. His biggest meal had been a litter of puppies he'd discovered in an abandoned barn, left neglected by their (dead or fled) owners. He'd downed them like bon-bons for breakfast.

Since then he'd eaten nothing but dry straw and insects.

At least until he'd reached Savenay.

He swallowed the mouthful of bandages he'd been

chewing. He'd stolen them from a man dying of gangrene, and had promptly sucked them clean of blood and pus.

His guts trembled and roared, merely angered by the fetid appetizer. He had to get something inside him or he feared his hunger would steal over his rational mind and force him to perform some outrageous act that would draw attention from the soldiers. He'd made it this far and had maintained control. He couldn't fail now.

Eventually he came upon the mass graves.

On the outskirts of the city, three trenches had been cut into a scorched, muddy field and filled with the dead.

Gaston walked along the edge of a trench, his heart pounding fast, his empty belly threatening to tear itself from his body and leap into the trench on its own, not having the patience to wait for chewing and swallowing.

The tangled bodies were caked with blood, clothes torn and perforated by grapeshot. A mass execution. Gaston's hungry, desperate eyes turned nervous and he scanned the surroundings to make sure he was not being observed.

When he was sure he was alone, he removed his knife from its sheath and jumped into the trench.

He scrambled over the bodies, sizing each one up like a greedy gourmand at a buffet. He finally settled on a plump young woman with a pale complexion, her body twisted into an awkward posture. He began to cut her clothes loose.

His mouth watered as her flesh was revealed, dropping small mucus pools across her stomach, filling her navel with his green/yellow saliva.

He was surprised (and shamefully delighted) to find

that her body was still warm. These poor souls had only recently been slaughtered.

Her fat, buttery thighs held the most appeal for him. He decided to save them for last and slid the knife into her abdomen.

She moaned and twitched and Gaston repelled backward as if suddenly burned, a terrified squawk rushing from his constricted throat.

Still alive! She's still alive!

Gaston scrambled out of the trench and began to run back toward the city, a horrified guilt consuming him.

His stomach stopped him.

His stomach turned him around and led him back to the trench.

He looked down. The wound he'd inflicted upon the woman was still bleeding. She did not move. He waited.

When he was fairly certain she was dead, he jumped back into the trench. His knife was still buried to the hilt in her side. With cautious, trembling fingers he pulled it free. She did not flinch.

Gaston began to drool once more as he started to cut.

Dead. She was dead this time. Thank God.

Gaston began to eat and his cruel stomach finally calmed.

As he stripped her bones, he loosened his clothes and unwrapped the loose flesh around his abdomen, filling his belly until it distended like an inflating balloon.

As his appetite became sated, Gaston grew drowsy. The long days of hardship finally came to claim him and he fell into a satisfied, comfortable doze.

When he awoke he found himself watched by a pair of hellish, yellow eyes.

"Monsieur," he said, surprised, trying to collect his stomach and get it back inside his now too-confining clothes.

The man staring at him was dressed in a uniform that appeared to be rotting off his skeletal body. He'd been burned hairless, his face seared and stripped of expression. He was lipless, his blackened teeth revealed in a terrible grimace. His eyelids had burned away, offering bulging, unblinking eyes. He held a rifle in his right hand. His left arm had been amputated at the elbow.

"I'm wounded," Gaston lied. "I was trying to get to town when I collapsed into this trench."

The man just stared, at both Gaston and the butchered corpse beside him. Gaston looked from the remains of his last meal to the soldier. "It's not what you think!"

The man just stared.

"She was dead! Already dead! You don't understand."

The man just stared.

"I am wretched, yes. But you must understand I am also cursed. Cursed with an appetite that does nothing but beg and scream like a spoiled child. You don't know what it's like! I tell you, it drives me mad!"

The man did not move.

"Why don't you speak? Have you lost your tongue? Please, just move, then, if you cannot speak. Make a gesture, nod your head if you understand what I'm saying!"

The man did not move.

"I didn't mean to kill her!" Gaston shrieked. "I thought she was dead! But I'm not a monster! I'm not! Yes, I devoured her corpse but her soul had flown on, that's the important thing. Who she was had gone, leaving all this meat behind. I was starving to death! What was I supposed to do? Let it go to waste?"

The man continued to stare at Gaston, as motionless as a scarecrow.

"Say something!" Gaston screamed at him. "Don't just stand there and accuse me! *Do something!* Kill me if you must but please do something! Anything!" Gaston began to cry, sobbing. Thick rheumy tears and snot ran down his twisted face. "Please, Monsieur... *kill me...*"

Thick fog began to swirl around the soldier and he vanished into the vaporous mist like the remnants of a dream.

Gaston, still sobbing, covered his face with his trembling hands and collapsed back into the heap of bodies.

When the men arrived to burn the dead they found Gaston still crying. He did not look up at their approach.

"This one's not dead yet," said one man.

The other man fired his gun into Gaston's brain.

"There," he said. "Now let's get to work."

NORMA RUTH FERGUSON
AND ST. ANTHONY'S FIRE

Hidden in the Ozark Mountains is an acre of cultivated rye surrounded by deep pathless woods. If you searched these woods, you might find a dead deer with splintered bone-shafts jutting from its fetlocks instead of hoofs – its crippled misery made apparent by its rotting posture. During the assaultive, suffocating summers, the woods are thick and primeval and the rye becomes weighted with fungal pods of ergot. In the center of the field is a black circle of scorched soil bordered by pointed stones. Many fires have burned there. If you happened upon this site, the first thing you'd notice is a change in the air. Despite the bright sunlight and calm sway of the rye, the atmosphere here is chilly and heavy and mournful. And if you walked over to the charred circle, the sudden change in pressure would pop your ears and trigger bitter nausea.

And if you were to dig through the damp ashes, you'd find bones.

Human bones, the bones of children.

On the morning of September 20th, Norma Ruth Ferguson discovered something strange on the steps of her trailer. At first she thought it was a football, kids were always losing toys around her house. There were two Frisbees and a wooden glider on her roof and a tennis ball in the gutter.

But upon closer examination, she saw that it was made of sodden brown paper, about the size of a cantaloupe, and egg-shaped. She scanned the other trailers with suspicion, a quick list of culprits tumbling through her mind. She knew damn well what the other residents thought of her.

Norma Ruth Ferguson was fifty years old and three-hundred pounds. She lived alone. Her husband, Garrett Emmett Ferguson died of liver failure in 97 and her daughter Cassandra ran away with her high-school guidance counselor six years ago and hadn't sent her so much as a *Don't-Worry-I'm-Fine* postcard.

Norma Ruth bent over – huffing and puffing – and lifted the soggy bag. It was light and delicate and fell apart in her hands, spilling hair, nail clippings and unidentifiable little pieces and shreds all over the steps.

"Honky-tonky Jesus!" she cried with disgust.

The hair that clung to her hands was sticky with a reddish-brown substance. *Blood!* she thought, backing into the trailer. She trundled to the kitchen sink and while she rinsed and lathered and rinsed and lathered she rifled through her list of likely culprits again.

"Bastards," she hissed between rasping gulps of air. "Dirty fucken bastards!"

She dried her hands and then collapsed into her wincing vinyl recliner to catch her breath and have a smoke. It was 7:30 a.m.

At 8:14, after a breakfast of two-dozen chocolate donuts, four cups of coffee, and three more Kools, Norma

Ruth returned to the front steps with a broom and dustpan and swept up the bloody hair, nails and god-knew-what-else.

Her trailer (a single-wide 1979 Commodore) sat at the outermost circle of the White Sun Mobile Home Estates. Behind it, a rusty chain-link fence bordered deep sprawling woods that stretched all the way to Missouri.

Norma Ruth threw the hairy mess over the fence, and then clanged the dustpan against a post to dislodge the stickier particles. Then she went back to her trailer.

For lunch she ate two boxes of Kraft macaroni and cheese, six hot dogs, a bag of Fritos and two forty-ounce bottles of Buckhorn malt liquor. Then she turned on Maury Povich and lit a cigarette.

She fell asleep before the first commercial break.

Six months before Norma Ruth Ferguson discovered the repulsive, anonymous gift on her steps, her daughter, Cassandra Hildegard Ferguson, gave birth to a girl.

She gave birth at night, outside, under a light rain.

Voices swirled around her; a loud, plainchant evocation rising to a crescendo as she grunted and wailed, arching her naked body. Philip, the child's father, was squatting on his haunches between her legs, working his fingers into the bloody dilation, pulling the root of her pain through the pelvic brim.

Cassandra inhaled the cool air, pushed, and then let her breath out in a long ragged scream.

The chanting stopped. She heard the baby squall.

Philip told her it was a girl. He told her not to worry and severed the slimy umbilical cord with an antique dagger. Mary helped her to a sitting position, slipped a pill into her mouth and then tipped a cup of water to her parched lips.

Philip gathered the tiny wrinkled infant in his arms, stood up, and then he and the others moved off toward the fire.

Cassandra fell back down and listened to the sonorous plainchant as the evocation was taken up again. She fell asleep listening to this. She did not dream.

The newborn didn't scream when Philip killed it. He skewered it on a spear of hickory and lowered it into the fire.

Norma Ruth Ferguson floated into groggy, hung-over consciousness and looked at the glowing orange numerals beside her: 7:02 a.m. She sat up with a moaning yawn and looked out the window. The world was swathed in thick sea-grey fog. "Holy dope-smokin' Moses," she groaned, forcing her heavy legs over the side of the bed with slow, laboring effort.

She lit a cigarette, lumbered wearily into the kitchen.

An hour later she sat by the window eating a package of bacon and a loaf of Wonder bread fried in bacon grease. Stubborn fog still clung to the ground as if anchoring itself against the tearing lift of the day.

The phone rang.

She struggled to a standing position, "Goddammit!" and picked up. "Yeah?"

"Hello? Mom?"

"Cassie?"

"Hi, Mommy."

It had been six years since she'd heard her daughter's voice and blood rushed into her head, making her dizzy.

114

"Oh my God, Cassie! Where are you?" Her heart was beating so rapidly she was afraid it might seize up and send her into cardiac arrest. Her hands were shaking. Six years.

"I just got into town. Can I see you?"

"Of course you can. My gosh! Are you okay? Cassie, are you all right?"

"I'm fine, Mom. I'll tell you everything when I see you. Are you gonna be around this afternoon?"

"Afternoon?" She couldn't think. What was she doing this afternoon? Then she laughed. "Yes, of course I'll be here this afternoon."

"Great. See you then."

"I love you, Cassie."

"Love you too, Mom. Bye."

Norma Ruth put the phone down and took several deep breaths. Lordy, lordy, Cassie was coming! She bustled into the bedroom to get dressed, brush her hair and paint her face. She looked a mess. She couldn't let her daughter see her like this! After six years!

Three months before Cassandra called her mother she was standing in a field of rye, deep in the Ozark Mountains. Sister Mary was lashed naked to a post, her blistered, truncated figure anointed and glistening with rendered deer fat, pasted with dried fibers of rye.

Cassandra held a short scythe and Father Philip, leaning on his crutch, recited the holy incantation.

The others, almost one with the darkness in their black rags, repeated his words with hissing whispers.

The fire crackled behind Mary, launching orange embers into the sky. She looked at Cassandra with dim rheumy eyes, awaiting her fate with lazy patience.

Cassandra had been Chosen. She had the Sight and would be spared from the solstice sacrifice for as long as she lived. Once a month, Cassandra was taken by the Spirit of the Woods. It struck without warning, making of her a violent apparition – foam-mouthed, convulsing, her eyes rolling into the darkness of her skull. She often awoke with a bleeding tongue, her muscles burning from her journey, and her mind transmitting the rich green language of plants that only her husband Philip could decipher.

Father Philip finished speaking and gestured toward Cassandra with the stump of his left arm.

She raised the scythe and slashed it across Mary's naked throat. The others began to chant. Mary gurgled and black blood bubbled from the new wound. Cassandra began to hack at her breasts and what was left of her disintegrating limbs.

Father Philip collected the meat to get it ready for the fire. Another feast had begun.

Norma Ruth sat chain-smoking all afternoon, eating Hostess Sno Balls, waiting for her daughter. When she finally heard a tap at the door her heart flinched and she pushed herself out of the vinyl recliner, her daughter's name on her lips before her nervous fingers touched the knob.

"Cassie..."

But this was not her daughter.

The woman standing before her was too old to be her daughter. She was haggard and thin and sunbaked, dressed in filthy, weeping rags, her hair long and wild and matted. Her eyes had the empty, faraway stare of a lost fanatic.

"Mommy?" the woman said.

"Cassie? Is that you?" And then she knew that it was and sadness and pity swelled heavily in her chest.

"Hi, Mom." Cassie smiled, showing a few green teeth. "Can I come in?"

Norma Ruth nodded, feeling dazed. "Yeah," she said, holding the door for her. "Of course."

"Thanks."

Norma Ruth didn't know what to say. She didn't want to hug her anymore. She looked terrible. She smelled terrible.

She noticed Cassie was holding a paper bag. "What've you got there?" she asked, remembering the horrid package she'd found on her steps.

"It's a present," Cassie said. "It's bread. I baked it myself."

Cassie reached into the bag and removed a large, dark loaf. She placed it on the counter. "You got a knife?"

"In the drawer there. So, um. How have you been? What have you been doing with yourself?" The questions sounded absurd.

Cassie began slicing the bread. "I've been good. Mmmm, you are going to love this. Butter?"

"In the fridge. Where are you living now?"

Cassie slathered butter onto two thick slices of bread. "Oh, here and there. We move around a lot."

"We? Are you still with that hippie guidance counselor?"

"Yes. Philip. We're married now."

"You're married? When did that happen?"

117

Cassie licked butter off her dirty thumb and then handed Norma Ruth a slice of bread. "Um, about five years ago."

Norma Ruth tried to hide her shock when she said, "Five years? You've been married for five years and you never told me?"

"Yeah. Sorry, mom."

"Why wasn't I invited to the wedding? Oh, Cassie..." She swallowed against tears.

"I don't think you would have felt comfortable at the ceremony."

"What? Why not? Cassie, you're my only daughter."

"Mom, try the bread."

Norma Ruth looked down at the slice in her hand. It was heavy and moist, almost black, peppered with strange seeds. "What kind is it?"

"....Rye....."

Norma Ruth looked at it.

"Go ahead," Cassie told her. "Take a bite."

Norma Ruth did as Cassie instructed. The bread was moist and dense and strong, but it was awful. It tasted like mud. The damp, fungal odor of rotting logs filled her sinuses. She thought of earthworms squirming under the clammy shade of a giant toadstool. She swallowed.

"Isn't that good?" Cassie asked.

Norma Ruth nodded. "M-hm."

"Have some more. I'll cut you another slice."

The second slice wasn't as bad at the first, but for the first time in her life, Norma Ruth actually had to force something down. She didn't want to hurt Cassie's feelings. Her tongue and throat felt numb, as if she'd been sucking a Novocain lozenge.

Cassie was smiling at her. "How do you feel, mom?"

"I feel..." *Cold, detached.* "I don't know how I feel," Norma Ruth said and laughed. She thought of the word, *upside-down* but shrugged instead of saying it. "Why?"

"No reason. More bread?"

"Okay."

By ten o'clock Norma Ruth realized she'd eaten the entire loaf. She felt a cold, bitter nausea in the pit of her stomach, but her head was warm and buzzed like bees.

Cassandra said, "Mommy?"

"Yes, Cassie?"

"Let's go for a walk."

"A walk?"

"Yes. I have something to show you."

"Oh. Okay. Yes, a walk. That might be nice."

Cassandra moved toward her mother. "Here, let me help you up."

"Thank you, Cassie."

Her stomach convulsed as Cassie helped her to her feet and for a second she worried she might vomit. The buzzing in her head grew louder and brief flashes of white light sparked in her peripheral vision. She could feel sweat cooling on her neck and forehead and began to feel drowsy.

She closed her eyes and a slow, heavy river of mud grabbed hold of her, carried her along on a thick, viscous current.

You okay, mom? The voice was a disembodied echo.

"Yes. Fine." She opened her eyes. They were outside, moving toward the woods. She gazed up and saw a full moon and the glittering wash of the constellations.

"This way, mommy..." Cassie took her hand and guided her forward.

Norma Ruth was blinded by the voyage. The ink-black darkness became a livid blackboard upon which her mind sketched spinning, ever-changing images. Strange faces with manic, melting expressions. Whirling, kaleidoscopic mandalas linked like tinker-toys across the jumbled canvas of her mind's eye. Her only bond to the solid world was her daughter's warm, guiding hand.

Just ahead, the wink of flickering lights appeared through the trees like giant fireflies.

Norma Ruth heard herself say, "Where are we?"

"We're here," Cassandra said.

Norma Ruth looked around. They'd entered an open field. Twelve robed figures stood around a bonfire. Each hooded stranger emitted a low droning hum. Cassandra let go of her mother. "Stand still," she told her. The humming ceased.

Norma Ruth didn't move as two of the robed, hooded figures moved toward her. They began to undress her.

She summoned the strength to protest. "Hey, no. Don't. Cassie..."

"It's okay, Mom. Let them do it."

The others stood mute behind Cassandra, watching, their faces expressionless shadows.

And Norma Ruth, who hadn't worn a bathing suit or even shorts since she was a child, and who was careful to avoid the stinging reflection of full-length mirrors, allowed them to remove her clothes, everything, and she stood naked and uncertain in the cool moonlight.

Another figure (a girl, Norma Ruth guessed) carried a small tin bucket over to her, dipped her hand into it and began to rub something hot and slippery over Norma Ruth's body. She dimly recognized the smell, and warm memories of her mother's kitchen drifted through her mind.

Another girl began to apply strands of straw to her slippery body. After she'd been covered with the hay, the girls limped back in line with the others.

Norma Ruth said, "What is going on?" in a pleading voice.

The strange congregation began chanting again and removed their robes.

"Honky-tonky *Jesus*..." Norma Ruth gasped.

Like leprous inmates of a medieval spittle-house, they stood naked before her, half-limbed and mottled with suppurating blisters, their expressions dazed and lunatic. Some possessed rounded stumps in place of hands or legs. Other truncated limbs ended in exposed, eroded bone, splintered and discolored. Some leaned on crutches, while others had fashioned crude peg-legs from planks of rough wood. One young man was nothing but a torso and he licked the sores on his swollen lips in anticipation of the ritual.

Norma Ruth tore her horrified gaze from this grotesque mob and looked to her daughter.

Cassandra was smiling, holding a shining scythe.

"Cassie? Cassie, please! I love you!"

"I love you too, Mommy," Cassie said and then she decapitated Norma Ruth with a single stroke of the scythe.

The motley congregation bowed their heads and began to sing.

Father Philip limped forward with his carving knife.

Another feast had begun.

AMY'S ARMS

We're sitting in the basement, drunk again. The coffee table is cluttered with beer cans, a bottle of Jameson whiskey, and her awful diet Sprite. I drink in chased shots. Amy drinks a mix of whiskey and warm flat diet Sprite.

I look at the red, lateral scars on Amy's arms, and say something – more to myself than her – and forget it. I suffer instant amnesia but whatever I said, it gets her yelling and her face is a twisted grimace and it strikes me as funny and I laugh.

She doesn't see the humor.

She stands up, shrieking and swearing, and I'm trying to figure out what I said but I can't stop laughing.

"Stop laughing!"

She grabs a badminton racquet and wields it like a weapon, like a samurai sword, and I still can't stop laughing.

Wap! She hits me in the face with the racquet.

I stop laughing.

Wap!

I keep smiling and lean into her.

Wap!

123

I want her to blacken my eyes, break my nose, knock out my teeth.

Wap! across the nose and I feel the blood start. I let it run over my smile, staining my teeth. I let it ruin the front of my shirt.

She drops the racquet. "Oh! Oh, I'm sorry. I'm so sorry baby..." She finds an old rag and presses it to my nose. "Lean back," she tells me.

"I'm okay," I say.

She hugs me and says she loves me and when my nose stops bleeding we sit down and have another drink.

That was so many years ago, it's excruciating to think about. The memory reminds me I'm gonna die.

Like Amy.

She died in a bathtub of warm water.

She used her old friend, Mr. Razor Blade. And this time, she meant it.

The radio was on when they found her. It sounds stupid but I wonder what song was playing as her veins emptied and the water clouded red.

I hope it was something beautiful and not some dumb DJ or obnoxious commercial. That might have messed-up her soul, cheapened it as it drifted into the water and up.

I don't go to the wake because I can't face her family and because if the casket is open I might scream.

I don't go to the funeral because I can't face her family and because when they lower her into the ground I might throw-up.

Amy, so long girl. I still can't remember what I said that day.

THE WET SPOT

The door opened. Pale desert sunlight seeped into the darkness of the Wet Spot.

As soon as the bartender saw the guy come in, he made himself alert. The guy looked like trouble. You develop a kind of ESP in a dump like the Wet Spot. You have to. Just about everyone who comes in looks like a badass or a nut or a gun-packing troublemaker. Most are just harmless, good-old-boy shitkickers looking to grab a quick buzz before heading home from work. But there was something different about this guy. Oh, he didn't really look that unusual. He was around fifty, gray hair spilling over broad shoulders, kept out of his eyes with a grimy red bandanna. His jeans and denim jacket were worn thin and white. His face was brown, baked with deep crags, haggard and falling from a lifetime of defeat.

But there seemed to be something wrong inside him. The bartender could tell by the way he moved. He creeped, as if trying to sneak into the place. His mouth trembled and worked, muttering to himself.

And those eyes.

The guy looked around the joint, once, twice, a third time, before he approached the bar. He sat down as if slipping into a tub of scalding water, face pinched with pain, breath coming out in one long gust.

The bartender approached him. "What can I getcha?"

"A beer," John said, pulling a wallet out of his back pocket.

"What flavor?"

"Whatever's cheapest."

The bartender turned, grabbed a mug. He kept his eyes on John the whole time.

John looked at the woman three stools down. She was drinking whiskey, her face obscured by a haze of cigarette smoke. She looked like an assassin.

A cowboy at the other end of the bar was staring at him, long oil-stained fingers wrapped like tentacles around a bottle of Bud.

The bartender placed a mug of beer in front of him. John plucked six bucks from the wallet he'd recently acquired from an old man he'd met at a Citco station, placed them on the bar.

He took a sip of beer. Cold. Ice cold. Nice.

"Hey, there, uh, buddy... Where you comin' from? Vegas?" said the cowboy.

John turned. The cowboy was tall, long brown hair pulled back in a greasy ponytail, mouth hidden behind a formidable mustache.

"The desert," said John.

The cowboy laughed; a dry husking sound. "No shit. We're *in* the desert, man. That ain't a proper response."

John shrugged. "Well, that's the only response you're gonna get." He took another sip of beer. The bartender was still watching him. He looked too small and jumpy to handle the kind of violence a place like the

Wet Spot must conjure up. He probably kept a shotgun under the bar.

The cowboy moved a few seats down. Only one stool separated him from John now. John kept his eyes on his beer, watching the bubbles climb into the foam.

The cowboy leaned toward him, wobbling. "Whussamatter? You think you some kinda tough guy or something, sayin' that?"

John looked into the cowboy's red-veined eyes. Dumb drunk eyes, no faking that. He was too stupid to be an assassin. Too stupid to be a real cowboy, even.

"No," John said. Ten years ago he might have started something, shoved something sharp and jagged into his dumb animal face. But he was tired. Too tired. "I told you the truth. I came from the desert. I live there. I do my work there, like John the Baptist."

The cowboy didn't say anything for a few seconds while he slowly unscrambled what John had said.

Out of the corner of his eye, John saw the woman turn toward them.

Gotcha.

The cowboy smiled. He was managing to hold on to one jutting bottom tooth. "John the Baptist, huh?" He laughed uneasily.

"That's right. The desert can teach a man a lot about himself. A lot about how things work in life. A barren landscape cleanses the mind. You should try it." He finished his beer.

The cowboy laughed. "Alright. John the Baptist. Or can I call ya Johnny? Fuck it. Okay, you came from the desert. Hey, Davie, why dontcha baptize John here with another beer. On me."

The bartender reached for the mug but John waved him back. "Don't," he said. He knew better than to accept a drink from a stranger. He'd been poisoned too many times. Too many people wanted him dead. "That won't be necessary. I'm leaving." He tossed another buck on the bar, thanked the bartender, and walked out. He didn't look at the woman.

The cowboy snorted. "What a fucking nutcase. You see his eyes? *John the Baptist*. Shit..." He lurched back to his stool, finished his beer, and ordered another.

"You leavin' too, Angie?" asked the bartender.

Angie closed her purse, stood up, and smoothed down her skirt. "Yeah. Gotta get back to work."

The cowboy laughed.

John was standing by his truck, watching the crimson sun sink toward the horizon. He could hear the assassin giving a splendid impression of clumsy drunken footsteps on the gravel behind him.

"What do you want?" he asked, without turning around.

She wobbled up beside him and slipped her arm around his waist. She was at least two feet shorter than he was. He could see the top of her pale scalp through her short black hair. The smell of heavy perfume, cigarette smoke and whiskey swirled into his head like poison gas.

"Thought you might want a little company," she said, purposely slurring her words. "You look lonesome. Am I right? I can tell by your eyes, you have..."

"I am not lonely," he told her.

He felt her stiffen under his arm.

She cleared her throat. "What a gorgeous sunset," she said, unsure of herself now.

Enough. "How much?"

She stiffened again. "How much what?"

"How much for access to that little pussy of yours?"

She broke away and a look of shock took over her pudgy, sunburned face. "What?" she said, like she was offended. He almost laughed.

"That devil's triangle you got between your legs. That *is* what you're offering, isn't it?" he said.

Her face turned to brick. Her eyes narrowed. "Twenty-five," she said.

"That's what I thought." John lifted the wallet and handed her two tens and a five. "I got a mattress in the back." He lowered the tailgate and climbed inside.

He slipped his hand over the shotgun behind the mattress.

Angie crawled in and kneeled on the mattress. She started patting her sweaty hair into place.

"Okay, John the Baptist, let's see wh..." She looked around then, really *looked* at the inside of his truck for the first time. Her eyes widened and filled with fear.

"What the fuck..."

Beautiful. What an actress. "What's wrong?"

Her face had drained of color. She opened her purse, snatched out the money he'd given her and let it fall on the mattress. "Nothing," she said. Her voice had gone small and breathless. "I just changed my mind is all." She started to crab-walk backwards, giving John a clear view up her skirt. "I gotta get going is all," she said.

John raised the shotgun. "Stop."

She stopped.

129

"Throw your purse over here."

She did.

He dumped out the contents. As usual, she knew not to carry anything that might give her away. She had exactly the kind of stuff you'd expect a woman of her age and type to have. But it was *too* perfect. Her cover rang as false as a dinner bell at the crack of dawn – pictures in her beat-up wallet of dirty children and long-haired men with sleazy, lounge-lizard mustaches. A pink heart keychain that said Foxy Lady. An old pack of Trident, wrapper faded and sticky with age. A new pack of Parliament menthol lights. Used tissues, condoms, crumpled receipts, a nub of a pencil…

But at least she had a few bucks. *They* were certainly real. He pocketed thirty dollars and some loose change.

"Can I please go now?" she said, little polluted rivers of mascara running down her cheeks.

"Yeah, sure. And tell your bosses that they're never gonna get another shot at me," he said, caressing the shotgun. "I am AWARE twenty-four hours a day. I DREAM them in my sleep."

She nodded. "Okay, sure, I'll tell them." She lowered the tailgate with shaking hands.

"I have been BAPTIZED!" he shouted.

She screamed and scrambled out of the truck, nearly tripping over her feet and spilling into the gravel.

John crawled out of the truck in time to see her run back into the Wet Spot. He hopped into the cab, twisted the engine to life, stabbed it into gear and sped back to the road, spinning clouds of dust and a hail of gravel behind him.

When he was deep inside the desert, he pulled over

and climbed into the back. He needed to pray and meditate.

He looked around at the inside of his holy sanctum. The walls were lined with animal skins and bones: steer, dog, cat, human. Fragmented skulls, X's made from long thin femurs, and clackity mobiles of polished bone. His headboard was an altar – two human skulls mounted on either side of a big plastic heart wrapped in barbed wire.

He tucked himself into the lotus position and tilted his head back to loosen the cramped muscles of his neck.

On the ceiling was a huge collage of pictures he'd collected over the years: car crash victims – blood and brains bursting from crushed, misshapen heads, gaudy, colorful autopsy photos of flayed corpses, innards exposed, genitals riddled with dripping syphilis, Thalidomide children, grainy, black and white photos of withered bodies stacked inside concentration camps, a scrapbucket full of bloody fetuses, women eating shit and drinking piss, men with their bloody scrotums nailed to sawhorses; women sucking off dogs, horses, pigs, getting fucked by apes, men pulling their anuses so far apart you could fit a cantaloupe inside, grossly deformed men fucking drooling, retarded children in the ass, women crushing kittens and puppies to death under fancy, elegant high-heels. In one picture a man with a stoned, gold-toothed grin is sticking his dick into a dead woman's jellied eye-socket, looking into the camera like a proud fisherman. Skull-fucking they call it. What'll they think of next?

He slept on his back and every morning, when he opened his eyes, this was the sight that greeted him. A mad vicious scramble of humanity.

131

Humanity as it really was. Beautiful and fevered and lost and fucking and killing their way into Hell.

He wanted to bless them all under his divine hands.

THE MAN WITH
THE BIG PANTS

October 24th, 1987

It was late and the man with the big pants was waiting for her. He stood beside the doorway to Rexall Drugs, trying to stay out of the late autumn rain. He could feel the cold, rough bricks through his thin wind-breaker and he held his coffee cup with both hands, trying without success to keep warm. He'd bought the coffee only five minutes ago – not even – and it was already going cold. Shit.

"Shit. Shit fucking motherfucking shit," said the man with the big pants. Where was she already?

The man with the big pants had quit smoking two days ago and right now he could strangle someone for a cigarette. He was quick to anger now that he was a non-smoker. And everything took too long - cooking, commercial breaks, lines, conversations. The night took forever. Everything was annoying now that the man with the big pants was a non-smoker. He took a cold sip of coffee. Shit, it was cold.

A woman bustled out of the Rexall, her arms full of fluttering plastic bags. Christ, what'd she buy – the whole fucking store? She dropped one of her bags and cursed under her breath. It landed by the man with the big pant's feet but he didn't bother to bend over and pick it up for her.

Nah, fuck you, thought the man with the big pants. The woman picked it up herself, juggling all her bags, muttering. The man with the big pants hoped she'd fumble and drop more, but no, she managed to gather them all. She cast him a shitty look – a slap-worthy look, really – and then waddled off into the rain.

Good, get lost, you fat old twat, said the man with the big pants, not out loud.

The man with the big pants shifted from foot to foot. He looked in the drug store like a hungry dog, at the vertical rows of cigarettes behind the counter. Where the hell was she? He wasn't going to wait in the cold and the rain and the elements much longer, that was for sure. He wouldn't wait forever.

Headlights splashed through a puddle – refractions of wet light ahead of him – and then her car was there. The man with the big pants tossed his cold, half-full coffee over his shoulder and walked to the car. The door was locked. He waited a second and tried it again. Still locked. Oh, what the fuck! He moved to the driver's side door. She rolled the window halfway down.

"Hey, Linda," said the man with the big pants. "How are you?"

Her face did not look happy. Her eyes were dark, angry, her hair in disarray, sticking up like she'd just tumbled out of bed. She wore no makeup. She didn't answer his question.

The man with the big pants said, "Hey, could you let me in the car?"

"No."

"But it's raining like a motherfucker out here."

"I don't care. Do you have it?"

"Couldn't you just let me in the car? I'm getting soaked out here, look at this shit..." He lifted his hands and tilted his head back to indicate that it was raining on him.

Linda shook her head. "You're lucky I'm here at all. If it wasn't for Tina..."

"Leave her out of it."

"You brought her into it. Do you have it?"

"Yeah, I do. I do have it, just open the door and I'll..."

"No. You're not getting in this car."

"Oh, c'mon, Linda. It's not like I'm gonna, like, do anything or anything..."

"Just fucking give it to me."

The man with the big pants looked around the parking lot. "Shit." He pulled a small metal box from his jacket pocket. It was a box for storing decks of playing cards. It was black and white and a blue rubber band held the old tin lid in place. He handed it to her.

"*Thank you*," she said, a lacing of sarcasm in her tone.

"Okay, you have it now. I made good. Now can I get in?"

She made a face. "What the hell for?" She punched in the car lighter.

"Gimme a ride home?"

She laughed and lifted a cigarette to her mouth.

"Oh come on, Linda. It's fucking pouring out here. You want me to catch pneumonia?"

"Well, yeah. I do, actually." She lit her cigarette, took a deep drag. "That or rectal cancer."

"Fuck you."

She blew smoke in his face and said, "Fuck you too, asshole."

The man with the big pants punched her hard in the face, breaking her nose. It was a sudden surprise for both of them. Her cigarette fell and she sucked in a breath, "Uhn..."

He hit her again, on the jaw this time. The middle of her face was an explosion of dark blood. He punched her again on the left temple, and her eyes fluttered white and she flopped over the steering wheel.

The man with the big pants reached in, unlocked the door and shoved her over to the shotgun side. He took over the wheel and pulled out of the parking lot.

Linda murmured, "Stop it...stop... don't..."

"Just relax, sweetheart," the man with the big pants told her. "It'll all be over in a minute." And then he hit her again.

He drove with purpose, with clarity. He felt calm, confident. He noticed there was no voice of reason nagging him in his head and he took this as a positive sign. He also realized he didn't want a cigarette anymore and decided this was another good sign. He was doing the right thing.

The man with the big pants turned on the radio and drove toward the river listening to Boz Scaggs's *Lowdown*.

When Linda tried to sit up, the man with the big pants

136

punched the back of her head and told her, "Stay the fuck down!"

With both hands on the wheel, he noticed his knuckles were torn and bleeding, yet they did not hurt. Another good sign.

The McKenzie River was a dark, wide, sluggish thing that snaked through a labyrinth of old, stone mills for a good five miles before it emptied into the thick, oily cesspool of Lake Grundson. The man with the big pants stopped at an old, stone trestle – the timber bridge had rotted away decades ago.

He aimed the car toward the edge of the trestle, yanked up the emergency break, and then opened the door and pulled Linda back behind the wheel. She murmured something that made no sense and then fell silent again.

The man with the big pants reclaimed the playing-card box and stepped into the rain.

He moved to the back of the car, opened the box, and removed a stack of photographs. He lowered them close to the glow of the taillights.

Tina on Christmas morning, kneeling under the tree, showing off her new Cabbage Patch Kid, smiling with a missing tooth. The man with the big pants smiled back. Those stupid dolls caused riots in the stores. They came with actual birth certificates, didn't they? Fucking stupid.

Tina at the ocean, digging in the sand, her fine blond hair blowing into her eyes as she grinned up at the camera.

Tina and Linda posing in the back yard. Tina was wearing her new Brownie uniform. Linda wore a striped tube-top and cut-off jeans. She was holding a cigarette in one hand and a can of Pabst Blue Ribbon in the other. She always ruined pictures by making herself look unhappy.

The man with the big pants grunted and then placed the pictures back in the box. He walked around to the front of the car, shifted it into neutral, and then released the emergency break. Linda was still out cold.

He shut the door, locked it, and then reached through the window, grabbed the wheel, and started rolling the car toward the ledge of the trestle.

The ground sloped downward and as soon as the car had gained enough speed, the man with the big pants let go. He didn't realize he'd shut the door on the flap of his windbreaker.

The man with the big pants panicked and tried to wrestle his way out of his jacket. "Fuck..." When the car started over the edge, he dug his heels into the dirt, trying to tear himself free of the material. "Fuck!"

As the car tipped forward the man with the big pants relaxed, bent forward, extended his arms and the jacket slipped away. Linda and the car and his jacket plummeted into the river with a loud splash.

The man with the big pants thought, *Jesus Christ! That was close!* and then leaned over the ledge of the trestle.

He watched Linda's car sink into a black swirl of bubbles and ripples and steam.

And then it was gone, underwater. Only the two red eyes of the taillights could be seen, peering up like a polluted sea serpent.

And then the red eyes went dark, blind.

The man with the big pants stared at the black current for a while, feeling the cold rain on his face. He realized the box of pictures had been in the pocket of his windbreaker. Damn.

He waited, looking into the murk, until he was sure Linda had safely drowned. Then he turned and started back toward town. The rain had picked up, the wind too, and the man with the big pants cursed the world for the loss of his jacket.

He was at least five miles from home. He'd get pneumonia for sure. Fucking Linda, what a cunt.

But at least he had Tina, his darling daughter. She belonged to him now. She'd just turned thirteen and custody was now guaranteed.

Oh, what wonderful days lay ahead.

BLACK EYE GLUE

Hobbies N' Stuff
by
Beatrice Brown

Part XXII: Black Eye Glue

Hello Friends! As you know, last July I acquired another Norwegian child, Fridtjof. In September I noticed that Fridtjof's eyes had begun to leak a thick, black discharge, similar to melted tar. I thought it was another bacterial infection so I administered broad-spectrum antibiotics. These had worked to clear up infections with several of the other children, including Knut, Atle, Gjertine, Solfrid and Torvald. But the result with Fridjof was not the same.

Some of you have asked for more details regarding the terrariums. I keep all my Norwegian children in 5'X5' Lucite cubes. Ventilation is provided by a Friendly Air-Phloe KLP7000F ceiling duct filtration system which is a class II medical device – so I really can't fathom how any airborne microbes could have sneaked in there. I mean, the Friendly Air-Phloe System exceeds the engineering control sections from the CDC TB Guidelines (1994) and OSHA's TB Enforcement Policy (1996). Yet infections continue to plague me, taking a bit of the shine off of a fun and fascinating hobby.

When Knut had his little lung trouble (see my column, Breathing Like a Landed Bass, November, 2006), he cried as if he'd been consigned to the strappado (this may not sound like a big deal, but it does diminish the enjoyment I feel whilst browsing my N.C. collection, and it completely ruined my Halloween party).

Several readers have asked me about sanitation and suggested that this may be the cause of the infections.

Each cube is equipped with a small vacuum toilet. After every flush, a brief burst of ethylene-oxide gas is released into the cube. Some have wondered if this may have caused the respiratory problems I encountered with Knut. I doubt it, but I have lowered the dose just in case.

The scent of Air-Phloe's New Carpet is being pumped into the cubes at present (I decided to take a break from Crisp Lemon. I'm anxious to try the new Ferns-N-Pines and intend to purchase several F&P filters when they come on the market in December).

After my column, Burning Urine Interrupted my Tea-Party (April, 2007), many have asked about Solfrid and her bout with a "female plumbing" infection. I am pleased to report that the problem has been eradicated and she now pees without screaming.

Now then, back to Fridtjof. After I began administering Levofloxacin, the black discharge thinned in texture, but did not cease. So I increased the dosage. As of Wednesday, it has changed in color and now resembles watery beef gravy, but the volume of the emission has actually increased, forcing me to restrain him and lock his head above a drainage basin. Fridjof cannot eat and is temporarily blind and if these symptoms persist much longer, I'm afraid euthanasia may be indicated. Regular readers of this column know my feelings about this issue (see June 2005; A Little More Complicated than Flushing a Goldfish). I would really prefer not to have to deal with the headache of disposal so soon after Ragnhild's cumbersome departure.

Oh well, often the most difficult hobbies are the most rewarding.

Anyway, it's almost feeding time so I've got to run.

Happy hunting!

Hugs,
B.B.

ANALYSIS

We only saw him once, if at all. He seemed like a normal guy at first. Smart, professional. We'd heard about this new therapy he was practicing, a combination of psychoanalysis and other things.

His name was Dr. Hans Frichtenstille, the famous psychiatrist who'd almost married Thelma Todd back in the 30's. He was in old newsreels of the time. There were rumors that he was tied to organized crime and that he'd launched his own satellite in 1955 and used it in his work. The satellite was called OWEN which stood for Otherworldly Whirring Endogenous Neurotransmitter.

OWEN transmitted things straight to the brain.

We arrived at his office on a rainy Tuesday afternoon. The receptionist looked like Margaret Dumont. She smiled at us.

"Name?" she said.

"Bobo and Iko," we said.

"Ack, Ack?"

"Bobo and Iko."

"Ack, Ack, please take a seat." She scribbled scribbles on a leaf trapped to a clipboard.

We sat down.

We thought we smelled roasting bear. It took us nearly five minutes to ask, "Is that bear meat we smell?"

"Black bear meat."

A nurse slid through the door holding a piece of gray parchment scrawled with hieroglyphic squiggles. She was tall, with black hair and dressed in starched whites. Her hair was curled in whorls like frozen surf and fastened with gold barrettes. She looked like a stewardess. She looked like one of those women who give away free samples at the grocery store. She looked like Snow White and we wanted to wash her. We wanted to wash her clothes. We imagined suds and they almost appeared.

"Ack, Ack?" she asked.

We stood up and crossed the room.

"Bobo and Iko," we told her.

"Ack, Ack. Follow me."

She led us to a small white empty room. She shut the door and faced us. She had a mole. It was peeking blindly from her front pocket. She did not speak. The mole did not squeak.

We all looked at each other, except for the mole because it was blind. Or dead. There was a lot of white glare in the room. We thought the room needed a calendar.

Time passed.

And passed again.

The only sound was the hum of ventilation.

The time we spent in the room was a bowl of motionless red Jell-O. It was a broken fiddle string. It was a wet chipmunk freezing to a tree. It was a bloody tooth wrapped in a Kleenex.

We stood like that for ten long minutes, and then she glanced at her bare wrist and said, "The doctor will see you now, Ack, Ack."

We followed her out of the room.

The hallway was paved like a sidewalk. Someone had been playing an extremely complicated game of hopscotch there.

The nurse opened a door and we entered the doctor's office.

Soreness soaked into our bones like lard in an artery.

A slab of bear-meat turned slowly on a spit above a huge humming space-heater. We noticed several tuna steaks and flounder filets mounted on plaques on the walls. Each one was dated. The carpet was foamy, like breakwater, and seemed to swell and eddy.

Dr. Frichtenstille had been stroking the neck of a gazelle behind his desk and he stood up. The gazelle settled to the floor, making a sound like a hinge.

"Ack, Ack?" he said.

"Bobo and Iko."

"Please, be seated," he said in an accent thicker than mud and toothpaste.

We sat down on a black leather couch. It squeaked in a way that the mole hadn't.

"Now then," he said. "I understand that you are abnormal."

"Eccentric," we said.

"Ah yes, eccentricity. The last refuge of the inventory clerk." He reached behind his desk and pulled up two large beer steins. "Mead?"

"Don't drink," we told him.

"Anymore."

"Anymore."

A black telephone on his desk began to ring. It rang six times before he said, "Would you like to answer that?"

"No thank you."

"It might be for you."

"No."

He picked up the phone. "Yes?"

He hung up. "It was for you. Your mother is dead."

The nurse entered the room carrying a pink plastic bucket filled with soapy steaming water and a scrub brush. She placed them on the floor and began to disrobe.

The doctor said, "I understand you'd like wash Ms. Pinhole."

We nodded, staring at her now-naked form. She winked at us and licked the corner of her mouth. Her tongue was Popsicle blue.

"But before you do that. Tell me about your dreams."

"We don't dream."

"I'm sorry, *We*?"

"Yes, us. We don't dream."

The doctor furrowed his brow. "Forgive me, but just who is *us*?"

"Us. Bobo and Iko."

The doctor shook his head with swift pity. "My dear boy. You are only one person."

"What?" I said.

"I think we've just made a breakthrough."

ATTACK OF THE
GIANT REPTILES

The MONSTERS are in REVOLT ...and The World is on the brink of DESTRUCTION! – Destroy All Monsters (AIP 1969)

"We didn't know why it happened or how. Everyone just had to react. Fast." – Me, years after The Event.

-1-

With civilization crumbling around us, we started ransacking Alice's house, gathering as much stuff as we could reasonably carry. I was rummaging through her cupboards and pantry, stuffing food into a Day-Glo Thundercats backpack. Alice hadn't gone shopping since The Event (nobody had – how could we?) and she didn't have much in the way of non-perishables (the perishables having perished days ago). Audrey and Phoebe were looting the rooms looking for weapons, while Alice gathered cherished personal items that she just couldn't part with (Alice being a soft, sentimental soul).

Audrey jogged into the kitchen while I was stuffing saltines and Ritz crackers into the pack.

"I found a machete," she said, dropping it on the counter.

"Alice has a machete?" I said.

She lifted the machete and dropped it on the counter again. The sound it made said, *Duh!*

"Keep looking. We should all carry something. We have to be able to protect ourselves in case we get separated," I told her, trying to sound like I knew what I was talking about.

"Okay, Ray," Audrey said and then resumed the desperate scavenger hunt.

Phoebe skipped into the kitchen. "I found this!" she said, holding out a silver color-guard baton, white rubber tips on each end.

I shook my head. "I said to look for *weapons*. What the hell are you gonna do with *that?*"

She began to twirl the baton, tossing it into the air, spinning it through her legs.

"That's real impressive, Phoebes, but it's not gonna scare off a gang of bandits with semi-automatic weapons," I told her.

Still twirling the baton, she said, "I could conk someone over the head with it."

"That thing wouldn't even raise a bump. Keep looking."

"Maybe I could modify it to make it more deadly."

"Keep looking."

She tossed it and caught it, still spinning, and skipped away. I stuffed Stove-Top stuffing into the bag.

Audrey returned to the kitchen, placed a small

chainsaw beside the machete and then left to continue her search.

Having cleaned out the cupboards (leaving behind only a pouch of microwave popcorn, bay leaves and a bottle of malt vinegar) I moved into the living room to find Alice stuffing pictures into a Rainbow Brite duffel bag.

"We have to get out of here," I said.

"Just a minute," she said, looking frantically around the room. She grabbed a framed portrait of her high-school self from the wall.

"You're taking pictures of yourself?" I said.

"I won't remember what I used to look like!" she said, her voice high and on the edge of hysteria. "Everything I own is about to be destroyed!" Tears welled shiny in her bloodshot eyes and I decided to shut up.

Phoebe bounced into the room carrying a baseball bat.

"What about this?" she asked, uncertain.

"Better," I said and I gave her an encouraging nod and a smile.

Audrey returned empty-handed. "I can't find anything else."

"We need one more thing," I said. "We should all carry something."

Alice said, "What about the shotgun?"

"Shotgun?" said Phoebe and Audrey in unison.

Alice stepped forward, reached above the fireplace and brought down a pump-action Remington 870 from the wall.

She tossed it into my startled hands and then patted two boxes of shells on the mantle.

I looked at Phoebe and Audrey. Phoebe lowered her

149

eyes and Audrey shrugged.

"Oh, Christ!" Alice said, slapping her forehead. "I forgot something." She ran upstairs.

"I have to pee," said Phoebe, heading to the bathroom.

"Hurry up," I said.

"It's only pee!" Phoebe yelled from the bathroom.

What did *that* mean?

Audrey had gone into the kitchen.

I don't know what possessed me to move to the front door and look out the window – some preternatural instinct or maybe just dumb luck.

I saw them.

Trudging toward the house were four men and a woman, all toting guns, heavy sacks slung over their shoulders. Scavengers.

Oh shit.

"We have to go! Now!" I screamed into the house, angry that the girls had separated into different rooms. I cracked the shotgun. Empty! "Now!" I ran to the fireplace, opened a box of shells with a shaking hand. "Now! Go! Now!" The air crackled around me, I felt dizzy, sick, as if I were collapsing into myself.

I loaded the gun just as the door crashed open. I fired both barrels toward the intrusion. The girls finally staggered wide-eyed and worried into the room. "Grab your shit!" I yelled. "Out the back!"

We scrambled to collect our things. I figured the gang of scavengers had taken cover and would remain hidden for at least a few minutes. I stuffed the rest of the shells into the backpack and then we ran through the kitchen, bumping and stumbling into each other.

A shot exploded behind us just as we tore out of the

150

house, across the backyard and into the pine woods beyond.

From the depths of the sea... a tidal wave of terror! –Attack of the Crab Monsters (Allied Artists 1957)

"It was a really fucked-up situation. Nobody knew what to do. I was no survivalist, that's for sure. I read The Anarchist Cookbook in high school but couldn't remember a damn thing about it. I was pretty clueless. We all were..." – Me, years after The Event.

-2-

It started happening six months earlier. The first reported sighting occurred on a Carnival cruise. The ship was traveling from LA to Puerto Vallarta when several passengers spotted something moving alongside the boat, just beneath the surface of the water. Excitement sparked among the tourists as reports of a whale sighting spread through the ship. Armed with cameras and camcorders, the passengers flocked to the starboard side to catch a glimpse.

Startled gasps and a few screams pierced the air as the creature raised its head above the water and kept rising, lifted by an impossibly long neck, until it was nearly twenty feet above the ship's sidewake.

Then it turned over on its side, revealing two huge flippers, and splashed below the surface again.

Unlike the Lock Ness Monster, there was ample evidence that the creature existed, evidence that played endlessly on the TV news.

Paleontologists identified the creature as a Muraenosaurus, a dinosaur thought to have been extinct since the Middle Jurassic Period.

It was all very cool and exciting.

For a while.

Only hell could breed such an enormous beast! Only God could destroy it! – The Giant Gila Monster (McLendon Radio Pictures, 1959)

"Of course we were scared! We were scared shitless! What kind of stupid question is that?" – Me, years after The Event.

-3-

Alice lived at the base of a mountain range and we literally headed for the hills. The band of scavengers didn't bother to give chase. It was the house they wanted.

I'd reloaded the shotgun and assumed the lead. "Keep your eyes open," I said. "A lot of people probably ran into the woods. Don't underestimate anybody. If they're desperate enough and hungry enough, they'll murder us just for the stale saltines in my pack."

"The saltines are stale?" said Phoebe.

"So, like, what's the plan, Stan?" said Audrey.

"I don't have one yet," I admitted. "But I'm open to suggestions."

Phoebe, Audrey and Alice were silent for a long time.

Walking was arduous – steep inclines, slippery leaves (it had rained that morning) and thick bushes and branches slowed our advance. We wound around jagged granite grades and thickets of thorn, losing time and our bearings.

"Hey, Alice," I said finally. "Are there any trails around here?"

"I don't know," she said.

"You don't know?"

"No."

"How can you not know?"

"I don't know. I just don't."

"How long have you lived here?"

"Around six years."

"Six years. And you don't know if there are any trails."

"How the fuck should I know? I don't hike. God, you can be such an asshole sometimes…"

"Look at this shit," I said, trying to push aside a thick wall of tangled, prickly growth. My hands and arms were crosshatched with angry scratches.

Audrey said, "Why don't you trade me the gun for the machete? That way you can hack out a path."

I stopped, turned. "Yeah, good idea. Here…" We traded weapons.

After two hours of excruciatingly slow progress Phoebe began to complain, trudging with heavy steps.

"I'm tired. Can't we break for lunch?"

"There is no lunch today," I told her. "When we make camp tonight, we'll have a small supper. We have to ration the food carefully. We can't afford to waste a single crumb."

Phoebe groaned. "But I'm tiiiiiired. And huuuuuungry…"

"Sorry, Phoebes."

"Why couldn't we take my Mazda?" she asked for the umpteenth time. I refused to explain it to her again.

When The Event happened, the roads quickly became clogged with panicked traffic jams. Road-rage turned to murder and sabotage – Molotov cocktails lighting up the night, impenetrable roadblocks of crashed and burning cars. Bandits with bulldozers began smashing cars off the roads and looting them, the passengers either dead or too damaged and dazed to put up a fight. Things had turned seriously Road Warrior after only a few days. Trying to travel by car was a pointless death sentence.

"Hoofing it is the only way to go now," I'd told her.

"This sucks," Phoebe whined. "Can't we at least stop for a snack? A little one?"

Audrey and I both yelled, "No!"

Invincible...Indestructible! What was this awesome BEAST born 50 million years out of time? – Reptilicus (AIP 1962)

"The whole thing was so weird, it turned EVERYTHING weird. The air was weird. I'd look at Alice or my sneakers or a cloud in the sky and it all looked like a surreal nightmare, like we'd stepped through a funhouse mirror into another dimension. Shit, maybe we had..." – Me, years after The Event.

-4-

The sky over New York City was thick with gray storm clouds when the first pterodactyl swooped down and perched atop the Empire State Building. It sat like a gargoyle on the Art Deco edifice, unmoving, its wet,

154

leathery wings folded over an enormous crouching body.

People stood and stared with dumb awe. Nobody panicked.

Yet.

Crowds continued to gather even as the rain fell.

Thunder erupted and the clouds behind the winged lizard blazed bright with lightning. It unfurled its wings and launched itself from its perch, plunging down in a screeching descent.

The crowds screamed and scattered.

A large, long-haired man in a *Frodo Lives* T-shirt – perhaps too terrified to move – was snatched by rib-crunching talons and carried skyward, while the screaming, fleeing people nearby were knocked to the asphalt by the powerful windstream gusting from the shadow of the lizard's vast, pumping wings.

A second pterodactyl descended through the clouds and began circling the city.

Then a third.

New York was under attack.

SEE the living, fighting monsters of Creation's dawn, rediscovered in the world today! – King Kong (RKO 1933)

"I was the guy, the dude, so I took control. Asserted myself leadership-wise. I figured it was my duty or something. Believe me, I could have done without the responsibility. I was terrified of making a mistake. Turns out I made almost nothing BUT mistakes. But, hey, none of those chicks volunteered..." – Me, years after The Event.

We stopped and made camp (such as it was) at dusk. We were exhausted, filthy and on-edge. Alice had owned next to nothing in the way of camping supplies: no tent, no sleeping bags, no lanterns or Sterno or a compass. She didn't even own a first-aid kit or length of rope.

"Why would I? I don't camp," she said.

"You lived in the mountains, in the middle of miles and miles of gorgeous forest for *years* and you never went camping once?" I said, annoyed.

"No. I lived in a house, genius. Why would I *camp?*" she said and then her face fell. "*Lived,*" she murmured. "I *lived* in a house." She began to cry, her casual use of the past-tense suddenly striking her.

"I'm sorry, Alice," I said.

We stood there for a long while, listening to Alice's soft sobs, avoiding each other's eyes.

Eventually, I clapped my hands and rubbed them together, trying to inspire. "Well, let's gather-up some kindling sticks and logs and stuff and get a fire going. Don't stray too far though. I don't want anyone getting lost."

I prepared dinner that night. Our only cookware consisted of one small frying pan and I held it over the fire, using a T-shirt as a potholder. We crouched like cavemen, watching, waiting for the Beefaroni to boil.

Alice was the only one of us who'd thought to bring silverware: one spoon (it was her baby spoon with her name engraved on the handle). We sat gathered around the hot pan, passing the small spoon around the starving circle. Audrey had doled out two saltines to each of us.

We ate without speaking, without joy. And when we were done, we were all still hungry.

Then Alice wrestled a baggie of pot from the pocket of her jeans.

This was the day that engulfed the world in terror! – The Deadly Mantis (1957 Universal)

"You know how in all those old giant monster movies, the military is called out to deal with the situation? Well, where were they this time? I heard about a couple of little, ineffectual skirmishes but for the most part the entire military-industrial complex was MIA. Shit, didn't they see it coming? Didn't the Pentagon have contingency plans for dealing with dinosaurs returning to earth? I mean, get REAL..." – Me, years after The Event.

-6-

The term, "The Event" is generally used to describe the one tragic day when all hell broke loose. Everything had been leading up to it but no one saw it coming.

It was Memorial Day, May 31st.

The question everyone asked was, Where did they come from?

The question was asked when a herd of Triceratops stampeded across Boston, shattering and flattening everything in their path. There must have been hundreds of them.

Where did they come from?

The question was asked when several Tyrannosaurus Rex appeared on the streets of Cleveland, snapping up pedestrians and ripping open overturned cars like tins of Spam.

Where did they come from?

It was the question asked when at least twenty brontosaurus were spotted grazing in the Everglades, when hundreds of feathered velociraptors swept into Washington DC, tearing apart anything that moved.

Where did they come from?

Whenever a Stegosaurus smashed open a home or an allosaurus ate livestock, the question arose:

Where the fuck did these fucking things come from?

FANTASTIC! ...the Allosaurus, alive in the twentieth century. – The Valley of Gwangi (1969 Warner Bros.)

"We didn't know how weird things had really gotten until we got to the top of the mountain." – Me, years after The Event.

-7-

We heard music in the trees.

We'd been climbing all morning, the incline growing steeper with each step, the terrain changing from damp thicket and soft, leafy soil to dapple-gray rock and dry lichen, the trees shrinking and thinning, turning to birch. The air was cool and sharp.

We had almost reached the summit when the chanting began – long and low and wordless. Flat, clumsy drumming accompanied the wailing choir.

Phoebe looked scared and grabbed my hand. "What's that?" she said. "I don't like it."

I just shrugged, listening. "I don't know."

"I don't like it."

"Me either," said Alice."

"Let's go back," Phoebe said.

"Go back to what?" I said. "Come on. Let's check it out." I turned to Audrey and held out the machete. "Here, trade back." She took the machete and handed me the shotgun.

We continued to climb. The chanting grew louder.

To finally get to the top we had to hoist ourselves over a boulder.

And there they were, around twenty people standing in a circle, howling, naked, and shivering in the wind. Three others, also unclothed, were pounding out disordered rhythms on a hollow log, pounding on it with thick sticks.

An old man stood in the center of the circle, arms raised, eyes closed. He was the only one attired – he had fashioned a long, flowing robe from a blue floral bed sheet. It flapped and waved in the wind.

Behind them, several small tents had been erected.

The old man slowly opened his eyes and saw us. He halted the concert with a gesture.

The now-silent circle broke apart. The nudists turned and stared at us. I turned to Phoebe and raised my eyebrows. She looked terrified and grabbed my hand again.

Alice gave the strangers a wave and said, "Hi."

The nude group nodded and several staggered Hi's and Hello's came our way.

At least they aren't hostile, I thought.

The old man in the bed-sheet robe stepped forward.

"Hey," he said. "Welcome to the Church of the Final Beginning."

"Thank you," Audrey said and taking her cue, we all thanked him.

"You're welcome," he said, smiling with big dingy dentures. "Have you come to join our little congregation?"

"Um," I said. "Actually, we didn't know anyone was up here. We were just trying to get away from the bandits. And, you know, the dinosaurs..."

"Oh, yeah. Smart." He waved his arms in a sweeping gesture. "Check it out, the last collapse of a civilization!"

I looked around. We could see for miles in every direction. Billows of smoke rose from the burning towns below. We heard the pop of far-off gunfire, the echoing roar of massive animals. I could see enormous reptiles thundering down lonely roads and crashing through trees – reduced to mere insect-size by our lofty perspective.

Three screeching pterodactyls wheeled and swooped around dense cumulous clouds, miles away.

It really looked like the end of the world.

The old man said, "So, you wanna join us?"

Phoebe said, "Do we have to take our clothes off?"

He smiled. His eyes were kind. "Whatever you're comfortable with, my dear."

"I'm more comfortable with my clothes on," she said.

"That's cool. Now, if you'll excuse us, we have a ritual to finish. Then, we eat."

The naked congregation circled the old man again and the chanting and drumming resumed. We sat down on the rocks to watch and wait.

The Giant Behemoth! The fire-spitting monster predicted in The Bible! – The Giant Behemoth (Allied Artists 1959)

"Fear does weird things to people..." Me, years after The Event.

-8-

Following the ritual, the old man – whose name, we learned, was Fenwick – ordered us fed. After his motley congregation had dressed, a large fire was started and they roasted three rabbits and a pheasant, turning them on an absurdly huge spit constructed from curtain rods, tent poles, bedsprings and several chains that looked salvaged from a child's swing-set. The spit was large enough to roast a moose. They also served us a watery pine-bark and mushroom soup. It doesn't sound very appetizing, but I regard it as one of the best meals of my life.

They passed us paper cups of bitter water ladled from a green plastic bucket.

I don't recall any of the church members drinking the water.

Afterwards, we all gathered around the fire. A large woman with thinning hair and burst vessels in her nose handed out two thin blankets to us, smiling with missing teeth. I shared a blanket with Audrey, while Phoebe and Alice wrapped themselves up together. The blanket smelled.

It was June but it felt cold enough to snow. I wondered if another Ice Age was dawning. Anything seemed possible.

Nobody spoke. We stared at the fire.

I don't remember falling asleep.

The next thing I do remember was waking up in a foggy dawn to the sound of Phoebe screaming.

I staggered to my feet, wobbling, dizzy, working to focus my blurred vision, trying to spot monsters in the fog.

Phoebe screamed again. "Nooo! Please no! Please! Please! Please! Noooo!" Another shrill scream.

I took a step, almost fell, and then forced myself forward. "Phoebe?" I called into the fog.

"Help! Over here!" Phoebe shrieked.

I finally moved close enough to discern what was going on.

A stocky man with a bristling beard cocked my shotgun and pointed it at my face. I froze and made a surrender gesture with my hands. "Don't shoot."

Phoebe had been strapped to the spit. The fire-pit below had been filled with kindling and stocked with logs. I caught a whiff of gasoline. A young girl stood nearby, holding a burning torch. The old man - Fenwick - was beside her, holding Alice's machete.

"What the fuck are you doing?" I said, stunned, trying to make sense of this terrible scene.

"God delivered you to us." the old man said. "He demands a sacrifice. Once he receives it, he'll keep us safe from the demons he unleashed."

I shook my head. "That's crazy," I said.

The old man nodded. "Maybe. But it's worth a shot."

A voice beside me startled me and I drew back.

"What's going on?" It was Audrey.

Alice joined us. "Hey, what the hell are they doing to Phoebe?"

Phoebe: "Help me!"

"They want to sacrifice her," I informed her.

"What?"

"They're gonna sacrifice her to God. They think that'll protect them from the dinosaurs."

"You gotta be shitting me," she said and stepped forward. The stocky man swiveled the shotgun toward her and she stopped.

"Please, don't do this! Please..." Alice said.

The old man said, "Too late..." and raised the machete over his head.

Phoebe screamed and he brought the machete down, severing the scream and her head. It tumbled off the spit and into the kindling.

Alice screamed and covered her face with her hands.

"Go ahead, Tiffany," said the old man. The young girl lowered the torch and the fuel in the fire-pit burst into an instant bonfire.

The church members began to disrobe.

They chanted and danced naked around the fire. Phoebe's skin began to sizzle and darken.

The stocky man with the beard smiled at us, then joined the others, waving Alice's shotgun in the air.

The old man was turning the spit. I could smell Phoebe's roasting flesh. I'm ashamed to admit that my stomach growled.

Alice and Audrey were crying. I grabbed their hands and pulled them away. We fled back down the foggy mountain, preferring to take our chances with dinosaurs and bandits.

No one came after us. I guess their god was satisfied with one sacrifice.

Poor Phoebe.

We hadn't gone far when we heard a piercing, ferocious roar behind us and then several screams and shouts. The shotgun fired twice. More screams, another roar.

The only thing I can figure is that the smell of roasted Phoebe attracted something big and hungry. As we stood and listened to the screams of the congregation, I couldn't help but laugh. I laughed for a long time.

Alice and Audrey didn't see the humor. They stared at me with disapproving looks.

But I couldn't help it.

Sometimes, even now when I think about it, it still makes me laugh.

JOURNALISM

<u>Norfolk, Va.</u> – In what may prove to be an elaborate hoax, citizens of Norfolk, Virginia have been scouring through the remains of animals killed on I-264, looking for clues to their futures.

Wal-Mart cashier Victoria Beane, who was among the first to discover a written fortune secreted within the innards of a rotted possum, claims, "It said I'd drink chocolate milk on Tuesday. And then I did. It's real uncanny. You can bet I'll be looking for more of them fortunes. I truly believe they were put there by God."

As a matter of public safety, Norfolk Mayor Paul D. Fraim has urged citizens to refrain from loitering on the highway and has stated that flinging small animals under moving cars is a crime, even if it may "supply answers to your destiny".

The Mayor further stated, "Sticking your hands in a decomposing raccoon looking for lottery numbers just ain't common sense. The people of Virginia should know better."

But Mr. Randall Fowler, an out-of-work iron-smelter, disagrees. "It's an uncertain economy and folks is [sic] looking for answers. S**t, I'll dig my hands in the belly of a sun-swollen, maggot-infested woodchuck if I think I might pull out the answer to my prayers. Or if it might tell me who I really am, real down deep like."

The fortunes appear to have been written on a manual typewriter on torn strips of yellow-lined paper.

So far, police have been unable to trace the origin of the fortunes.

"Whoever is writing these things and sticking them inside dead animals is sick," stated Norfolk police chief Bruce P. Marquis. "And he can't spell worth a damn."

Meanwhile, police have noted an increase in both traffic and pedestrian activity on I-264.

"Until this thing is solved," said Mayor Fraim. "We're gonna have a lot more accidents on the road. And a lot more flat animals. Heck, we're all interested in the future. But frankly, this is just sad. Just sad."

* * *

Padden, Me. – Ask 111 year old Agnes Baines Cooper the secret of her longevity and you're liable to get different answers depending on her mood. This morning, sitting on a faded settee by the window, she credits memories. "My memories keep me young," she says. "[They] keep me warm when it's cold and fill me up when I'm hungry."

Agnes was born May 16th, 1901 in Glenwood County. It was the year Queen Victoria died and Clark Gable was born; the year William McKinley was assassinated and Theodore Roosevelt became the 26th President of the United States.

When asked which moments in her life stand out in

her memory, she is quick to mention the time she danced with Fred Astaire. "I was living in Los Angeles at the time," she says, opening a jar of Vicks VapoRub. She dips a spoon into the mentholated jelly and swallows it down. "I eat a tablespoon of Vicks every morning. [It] keeps these old pipes of mine running smooth as a greased canal. Anyway, yes I danced with Fred Astaire once. Or was it Ray Bolger? I'm not sure anymore. It was one of the two."

Using a cane, she pushes her thin, wobbling frame out of the settee and says, "Let me show you my collection."

She moves slowly, arms trembling. The years and miles have taken their physical toll but her eyes remain bright and alive. She stops in front of an antique china cabinet. Behind the glass are rows of mason jars. The jars contain what appear to be clumps of dirt. Faded yellow labels are affixed to each jar with peeling, ancient tape.

There are names written on each label in neat, flowing script: Mabel Normand, Wallace Reid, William S. Hart, Lon Chaney, Gloria Swanson, Rudolph Valentino...

When asked what the jars contain, she grows wistful, lost in distant memories. "Bowel movements," she says without a trace of irony or embarrassment. "The exquisite excrement of shining, bygone movie stars."

When asked how she came into possession of such a strange, remarkable collection, Agnes replies, "I worked for a man who supplied the movie industry with certain things. I was a kind of courier, you might say. The movie stars were always excited to see me and most of the time they were gracious enough to give me what I wanted. Some were puzzled, of course, and my laws, did Mary

Pickford put up a stink! It took me three months to convince her to contribute to my collection."

She opens the cabinet and takes down a jar labeled with the name of silent swashbuckler Douglas Fairbanks. "These are pieces of history, the inner essence of beautiful, remarkable people. I believe every one of these jars contains a part of their soul."

She removes the lid and sniffs the chalky sediment. "It doesn't smell anymore," she says in a sad, cracking voice.

The old aromas have faded away, the once solid fecal matter crumbled to dust, much like the stars themselves, much like the memories of Agnes Baines Cooper.

* * *

Boston, Ma – Psychiatrist William Abrams will admit he is perplexed. Three patients have come to him recently with the same unusual problem; a belief that their hands are no longer their own.

"I've never seen anything like this," said Dr. Abrams. "They seem to be suffering from the same strange delusion."

Dr. Abrams, 62, has been a practicing psychiatrist for nearly forty years. Three months ago, a young man visited his office in Somerville. "He was referred to me by his primary-care physician," said Dr. Abrams. "He swore that several days earlier, he had awoken to find that he had someone else's hands. I have to admit, preposterous as it seems, his hands *did* look as if they belonged to someone else. He's a 23-year-old software engineer, but his hands were rough, callused, heavily lined, with dirty fingernails. They looked like the hands of a man who'd been doing physical labor for many years. It's very peculiar."

A few weeks later, a 32-year-old woman came to see him. "She was quite distraught and thought she was going crazy. She told me she was a lifelong nail-biter and then showed me her hands. She had long nails, perfectly manicured and painted with red nail polish. She told me her hands had changed overnight. She insisted she'd never worn nail polish."

But perhaps the most surprising case was the 56-year-old man who came to see Dr. Abrams several days later. "Again, it was the same story; his hands had been replaced while he slept. He now had an inverted pentagram tattooed on his left hand and an expletive crudely tattooed on the fingers of his right. This man told me that he was a professor of literature at Harvard and a deacon at his church. He swore he had never gotten those tattoos."

When asked his professional opinion of these cases, Dr. Abrams shakes his head. "I'm not sure. Ordinarily, I would classify it as a somatic delusional disorder. What's so unusual is that three people who have never been in contact with each other would share the same delusion."

But it isn't just Dr. Abrams who is encountering this strange phenomenon. Reports of people claiming that their hands are not their own have been popping up across the country. One woman in Wyoming went to the police with her concerns. "These are not my hands," she said in her statement. "They belong to someone else. Look at them. They're little kid's hands. And where did *my* hands go? Are they on somebody else? God knows what kind of disgusting things they might be touching and feeling right now."

When asked if an overpowering belief in this delusion might have caused his patients to physically alter their hands without retaining the memory of doing so, Dr. Abrams answered, "It's possible I suppose. I just don't know. Not yet, anyway."

* * *

<u>Clearhaven, Fla.</u> – Lupus Vulgaris, singer and lead guitarist of cult band, Bleak Holiday, dies at 48.

The pleading, urgent sound that Lupus Vulgaris (nee' Duncan Bell) produced with his group, Bleak Holiday, has assured him cult status among fans of "disease rock," and has influenced and inspired several bands, from Eruption of Smallpox, to Black Lymph.

Lupus Vulgaris was born Duncan Christopher Bell in 1963, in Fayetteville, Arkansas. His father was a research scientist and had played guitar in a bluegrass group, The Chewy Boots. Bell Sr. taught his son to play guitar and at 16, Duncan Bell joined a local band, Ludicrous Wobble.

Ludicrous Wobble scored a minor underground hit with the playful, new-wave song, "I Like Sneezing", but creative differences led Bell to abandon the group in 1979.

After dropping out of the University of Arkansas in 1981, Bell formed the band, F*** Your Mother, an in-your-face punk trio. The band recorded the hardcore anthem, "F*** Your Mother", in 1982. F*** Your Mother disbanded after six volatile months, releasing only one record, the six-song EP, *F*** Your Mother*, on their own short-lived record label, F*** Your Mother Records.

The next year, Bell legally changed his name to Lupus Vulgaris and assembled the band that would cement his legacy: Bleak Holiday. Their first album, *Sonnets from a Deathbed* (1983) was a gloomy, psychedelic affair that received little notice upon release. However, one track on the album, *In the Grippe of Influenza*, received airplay on several college radio stations and was a thematic harbinger of things to come.

Wholly embracing the disease theme on their second album, *Tubercular Tubers in the Garden of Disease* (1985), Bleak Holiday slowly achieved cult-status with such songs as, "Embrace Thee Smallpox", "I Have an Abscess", and "Gimme Typhus". The songs, all written by Vulgaris, combined dirge-like tempos, heavy-metal guitar muscle and pop melodies that would have been catchy if not slowed down almost to the point of disintegration (in 1997, proto crunch-pop band, Soothing Mucilage scored a top-ten hit with a speeded-up cover of "Gimme Typhus").

The success of the Tubercular Tubers album led to two years of constant touring and a string of misadventures and strange rumors that have since become legend. One such rumor, that band members had intentionally infected themselves with meningitis in order to spread the disease among their fans, continues to surface every few years among chroniclers of urban legends.

A third album in 1988, *Pancreatic Carburetor*, while popular with Bleak Holiday's hardcore fans, failed to take the band to the next level. Frustrated by a lack of mainstream success, tensions within the band, and Vulgaris's increasing drug dependency, Bleak Holiday disbanded in December of 1988.

In 1990, Vulgaris returned to the studio with punk producer, Dan "The Man" Port-O-san, to record a solo album, *Cultivating Chancres*. *Cultivating Chancres* included innovative but painful songs such as "Pus-Flood" and "Bed-Sore Collector". Receiving negative to hostile reviews, the album quickly disappeared.

Vulgaris dropped out of music after the failure of his solo effort and worked a variety of dead-end jobs in Florida, which was to remain his home for the rest of his life.

In the wake of renewed interest in disease rock, Lupus Vulgaris had planned to re-form Bleak Holiday, record a fourth album, and embark on a reunion tour. He died two days before the band was set to enter the studio.

Lupus Vulgaris, rock musician, born May 15, 1963, choked to death on a macadamia nut on December 25, 2011, aged 48.

STABLE

The man sat at the table, drenched in the dense California sunlight that burned through the glass patio doors – American sunlight – and he felt like an important part of an important moment. He was in this place now. He stirred his coffee and scanned his newspaper and felt satisfied. He felt proud of his house, his career. He loved his wife. He realized this with urgent clarity and a gratitude that usually eluded him. The sounds of Carol fixing breakfast in the kitchen comforted him, secured him to the world, and after a while the smell of bacon and toast traveled through the swinging door and he felt better still. It was a perfect moment, an *exact* moment, when the very molecules of existence seemed to coalesce and charge his darkening heart, a heart that had begun to harden and retreat from the anxious complications of impending middle age.

The newspaper was still filled with the recent tragedy. A great American had died in Dallas at the hands of a troubled young man, and then the young man was in turn gunned down by a man with a jeweled name who ran a nightclub. He wondered if he should feel so calm and contented so soon after a national calamity and with

173

this thought, the perfect moment was gone. One brief blaze of doubt had kindled it to mist.

The man felt diminished again.

The swinging door flapped open and Carol crossed the dining room and set a plate of fried eggs, bacon and toast in front of him.

"Here you are, darling," she said, beaming. When she smiled, her whole face smiled. The depth of her eyes intensified her expressions to the point of heartbreak.

"Thank you, dear," the man said, glancing up from his paper. She bent down, offering her cheek, and he gave her a quick peck.

"What are your plans for today?" she asked him.

"Plans," he said, then scooped a forkful of egg into his mouth.

"Yes, plans. What are your plans?"

"Exactly."

"Huh?"

"Plans."

She spoke his name in anger, her eyes transmitting sudden frustration. The bright smile had vanished.

He laughed. "I'm sorry, honey. I'm drawing up plans for the new art gallery they want to build downtown. So, I'm planning... to plan plans!" He laughed again and shrugged his shoulders, eyebrows raised in a way he knew she found cute.

But she didn't find it cute this time. "*Oooh!*" she said, giving voice to her waning patience and then stormed back into the kitchen.

He shrugged again and returned to his breakfast.

When the man finished eating he lifted his plate and coffee cup and carried them into the kitchen. Carol was standing at the sink, scrubbing the frying pan with brisk, angry strokes, her small, delicate hands hidden under Playtex Living gloves. The man came up behind her and kissed her gently on the neck. She stiffened slightly, still cross with him.

The man cast his eyes down and toed the linoleum like a repentant little boy. "Gee, I'm sorry honey," he said. "I was just kidding around. I woke up feeling playful today."

"Well, I'm *not* feeling playful today," she said in a firm voice, dunking the frying pan in the soapy water. Bits of egg-white floated in the foam and the man studied them as if they were keys to a dream.

His wife released a long, suffering sigh and the man wondered, not for the first time, why he felt driven to continually test her patience. Maybe he just couldn't understand what she saw in him, such a beautiful woman, and he needed to prove himself unworthy of her love by acting like an obtuse clown, a bumbling fool.

He cleared his throat and tugged his collar and when he spoke he hoped that his tone conveyed honest concern.

"What's bothering you, dear?"

She tilted soapy water from the pan and then dunked it in the clear water of the rinse basin. "Well, if you must know..."

"Yes?" he said, an eager inflection in his voice. But he knew from her prologue that he would not be getting the truth. She would complain about wanting a new dress, a fur, or a week in Hawaii. But he knew what she *really* wanted above all else. It was the cruel, desperate nucleus from which all the small, pesky little demands sprang.

He had been unable to give her a child for two years now and maternal panic kept her on a precarious emotional edge. When they were in town and a newborn in a stroller wheeled past, the pained, longing look on her face was enough to make his heart burst into soft fragments. Even now, without looking at her face, he felt a sickening mix of pity and guilt.

"Never mind," she said, slipping his yolk-smeared plate into the warm suds.

He thought of saying something cheerful, or cracking a joke, but he knew the gesture would only make her feel worse. He placed his hand on her shoulder, felt a nuance of tensed muscle, and then left her alone.

He stepped outside, into the backyard, the fresh air reviving him, gifting him with a faded filament of his earlier reverie. The little apple tree next door was dotted with blossoms, active with orbiting bees. The man still found it hard to believe that Roger, his neighbor and often-difficult friend, was gone. A military officer from the man's Air Force past had moved in not long after the funeral. A colonel. His old commander.

The colonel sometimes thought the man was crazy.

A lot of people thought he was crazy. He could see it in the baffled, uneasy expressions that sometimes confronted him. He knew what people said about him behind his back. He didn't care. He knew his grasp on reality was not tenuous. He was not clinging to sanity like a man in a roiling void. His sense of himself, of his life, was settled on a foundation of safe, unyielding bedrock. He knew this. Granted, he could act eccentric at times and circumstances necessitated a certain degree of secrecy, but he was not crazy.

The man entered a small stable at the edge of the backyard. His office was there. His best friend lived there.

"Good morning, Ed!" he said.

The horse was wearing glasses, reading The Wall Street Journal. He didn't look up when he said, "Mornin', Wilbur."

WORK

"I'm a craftsman," I kept telling myself. "An artist."

I confronted my job at dawn, my dread rising with the light. I worked outdoors and every morning I prayed for rain. We couldn't work in the rain.

The day was bright and clear.

I parked my dying Dodge Shadow under a catalpa tree, took a deep breath. Karen's upcoming abortion was still on my mind and I'd thought about calling in sick just so I could THINK.

I left the car with the tree and headed toward the fields.

It was early summer and the smell of the flowers was overpowering. Twelve acres of flowers and flowering trees, each little stab of color puffing perfume into the air. I'd been working at Addax's Art Nest for two months and already the smell had become cloying, noxious, headache inducing.

I walked across a worn wooden footbridge that forded a narrow stream they kept stocked with shy, timid goldfish. I glanced at my wrist and saw I still had a few minutes before I had to punch in, so I stopped mid-stream and looked down. The water was kept clean with a filter, the little river-bottom paved with perfect white pebbles. I didn't see any goldfish.

I stood like that for a while, looking at the calm, speckled current and the cattails and blooming milkweed beyond. I thought about Karen.

And then I noticed the buzzing – that hateful droning – and it wrecked things; the quiet, my daydream. I finished crossing the bridge and headed into the office.

Mr. Philips was sitting behind his sprawling, Polyester acrylic desk, smoking his breakfast-cigar and spreading fresh honey on a piece of burnt toast. He looked at me, then back at the toast. "You're almost late," he said.

I shrugged and apologized. Gertie and Dave were already there, drinking coffee, chatting. They were never almost late. They gave me synchronized nods of greeting. I nodded back and then filled out my time-card: Hank Kirton, Employee #24, and punched in. I was five minutes early. I slid my card into the rack and then approached Mr. Philip's desk to suffer my assignment.

He sucked his cigar and bit into his toast, slowly releasing smoke. He tossed me a photograph while he chewed. I looked at it – a small boy in red pajamas smiling in front of an ugly Christmas tree. His teeth were crooked. They overlapped.

The boss told me, "Kid's name is Robert. Died from a bad case of leukemia last year. His parents want his portrait done with his name underneath. Robert. Make sure you write it neat: Robert."

Calligraphy was not my strong suit.

I slipped the photo into my pocket and nodded. "What's the canvas?"

"Hornet. Tree 17. Get going."

179

"Hornets?" I said. Very few customers ordered Hornets. We sold a few to aging punks and pseudo-Satanists but most people wanted cute, peaceful bumblebees.

"Yeah, hornets," said Mr. Philips. "You gonna make me say `Get going' again, Kirton?"

"No, sir."

I walked behind the office to pick up my box of paints and a ladder. The stink of the garbage pile out back – collected from three local restaurants and used to attract and feed yellowjackets – was a welcome break from the smell of the flowers.

I grabbed what I needed and trudged into the jungle of blossoms, trying not to notice the buzzing wave of bees rising in my wake.

Tree 17 was a huge gnarled apple tree surrounded by goldenrod with the number 17 spraypainted on it. I looked up at the large, gray hornet's nest hanging from a thick limb, surrounded by angry black satellites.

I set up the ladder and started to climb.

This was my job.

The first sting hit before I reached the top – a fiery needle in my neck. I slapped the hornet, pinning it against my skin and then pinched it loose, grinding it to pulp with my fingers. I flicked most of it away, and then wiped shredded exoskeleton off on my jeans.

I climbed another two rungs until I was face to face with the nest. I placed my case of paints on the ladder's shelf and pulled the picture of ROBERT out of my pocket.

I looked at the dead kid and the ugly Christmas tree. A hornet landed on my forearm and I didn't move. I just stared at the picture. The kid was smiling but he had sad eyes. I wanted to capture those eyes. The hornet on my arm flew off without stinging and I began to sketch Robert on the nest with a thin piece of charcoal. I wondered if I should fix his teeth a little.

Another sting landed on my scalp and I tried to ignore it.

I suffered two more stings by the time I finished the sketch – one on my back and another on my neck. I could feel them starting to swell, turning to painful knots. The sun was shooting straight at me, making it hard to see, drawing out sweat.

Gertie's voice behind me: "How's it going up there, Hank?"

I turned. "Hey, Gertie. It's going okay, I guess. What'd you get today?"

"I got a dog." She held out a picture, flapped it and then looked at it, cocking her head. "I think it's an English setter or something."

"Where you painting it?"

"On a stingless honeybee nest. Heading over to the cave now..."

Stingless bees in a cool damp cave. Philips always gave Gertie the softest assignments.

"Okay," I said. "Good luck."

"You too," she said and then disappeared behind a wall of Rhododendron.

I went back to work.

By the time my lunch break arrived I'd collected a total of ten stings. None of them were around my eyes, unfortunately. If one of my eyes swelled shut I could go home.

After I'd dug the stingers out and cooled the wounds

181

with Caladryl, I sat in the break-room, watching bad-reception local news and eating a warm ham sandwich. Dave lumbered in and sat at my table. He sported a red, swollen bee-sting in the center of his forehead like a third eye.

"What's up, Kirton?" he said. He pulled a jar of pickled vegetables out of a paper bag.

I shrugged. "Not much. You?"

"Drawing a couple of newlyweds on a bee's nest. Should be done by four. It's fucking hot out there, man."

I agreed.

"What you working on?" he said.

"Some dead kid at Christmas."

"Dead kid, huh? You're lucky. You should see the fucken broad I gotta paint. Fat as an ocean liner. Plus all that fucken white lace detail on the wedding dress. Shit, man, we need a fucken union."

I chuckled. "That'll be the day." I took a bite of my sandwich.

Dave harpooned a carrot with his fork and plunged it into his mouth.

"No shit," he said, sighing and chewing at the same time.

After lunch I returned to tree 17. Clouds had begun to accrue, thankfully blotting away some of the sunlight. I ascended the ladder, reopened my paints.

Those eyes. Robert's sad eyes were an intimidating challenge so I saved them for last.

I started painting the ugly Christmas tree. I filled its shape out a little more, brightened the ornaments, replaced dry, dead branches with green needles.

I felt a sting on the back of my neck. Another hornet

buzzed into my cheek, ricocheted off and went on its way before I could slap it.

By the time I got to Robert's eyes, the rest of the painting was done. I studied the boy's face.

I tried to take a deep breath. The venom in my system was making me dizzy, nauseous, making it hard to breathe. Some days the venom-sickness got so bad, I threw-up my lunch. I tried to put thoughts of vomit out of my mind.

I started working on the boy's eyes. They were large and blue and wounded. I did the best I could.

When I'd finished, I leaned back.

I nodded to myself. The sadness was there. I'd done it. A hornet flew into my sleeve and stung my armpit and I squeezed it to death under my arm, still nodding at my accomplishment.

Mr. Philips would have to be impressed with my work this time.

I wrote the name ROBERT beneath the portrait in fairly neat gothic lettering.

And then the sky fell.

The clouds had turned a roiling purple and sheets of rain slammed down as if the sky were a bursting dam. I turned to look for one of the small plastic tarps we used to cover our still-wet work and then realized I'd forgotten to bring one.

The hornets had fled the rain and I watched Robert and the ugly Christmas tree begin to melt and run, turning to dripping rivulets of gray.

And then they were gone. Only a vague ghost of the image remained, like the shadows of Hiroshima victims scorched on cement.

I climbed off the ladder and shuffled back to the office, soaking wet. By the time I got there, the rain had stopped.

Mr. Philips was behind his desk, leafing through new pictures, new orders.

"You finish, Kirton?"

I nodded. "Yeah."

"So, the crew can pick it up in the morning?"

The crew. They were the guys who removed the finished nests and drove them over to the customer's home and installed them on the property. The crew got to wear beekeeping suits, gloves and a veiled hood. But then, they were union.

"Um, no," I said. "That rain came down so fast the paint got washed out."

Philips stared at me.

"Are you fucking shitting me, Kirton?" he said, red-faced.

"I'm sorry." I felt dizzy.

"WHY THE FUCK DIDN'T YOU COVER IT UP?!" he screamed.

"I didn't have time," I said. "That rain came out of nowhere..."

"No, it didn't come out of nowhere! It came out of clouds! What do we do when we see dark clouds, Kirton?"

I slumped. "Get a tarp."

"That's right. Jesus, you were supposed to learn that on your first day you fucking moron!"

I shrugged. "I'm sorry. I'll re-do it tomorrow."

"Damn right you will. And then you know what you're doing?"

I shook my head. I felt faint, sick.

"You're gonna stay late and you're gonna redo today's assignment AND do tomorrow's assignment. You gotta twofer tomorrow and you better get `em both done."

He tossed me a postcard. "Some art-history teacher wants this reproduced on a wasp nest."

I looked at the card.

It was the ceiling fresco, Glorification of the Reign of Urban VIII by Pietro da Cortona (1633-1639).

That's when I threw-up, all over Mr. Philip's Polyester acrylic desk.

After I cleaned up the mess and received another chewing-out from Mr. Philips, I staggered to my car. My vision was still too out-of-focus to drive so I just sat and waited for the venom to wear off.

It was only Monday.

About the Author: Hank Kirton was born in Arkansas in 1967. He lives and works in Massachusetts.

Apophenia is an imprint of
www.paraphiliamagazine.com

For information and to purchase other titles:
http://www.paraphiliamagazine.com/books.html

www.ingramcontent.com/pod-product-compliance
Lightning Source LLC
Chambersburg PA
CBHW072112170626
46813CB00004B/1509